JOHN'S JAM-PACKED JOTTINGS

D0994142

Alexa Tewkesbury

CWR

See back of book for list of National Distributors.
Unless otherwise indicated, all Scripture references are from the Good News Bible, copyright © American Bible Society 1966, 1971, 1976, 1992, 1994.
Concept development, editing, design and production by CWR
Illustrations: Helen Reason, Dan Donovan and CWR
Printed in Finland by Bookwell
ISBN: 978-1-85345-503-2

Greetings, diary dudes! It's me, John, and have I got some wicked stuff for you to read about! There's life with my twin sister, Sarah, for a start, which is definitely crackers but pretty cool (I'm cool, Sarah's crackers). There's also all the latest on my dog, Gruff, and Saucy, Sarah's cat. And as for the Topz Gang, you'll soon find out exactly what a FANTASMAGORICAL bunch of Topzies they are to belong to! If you haven't met us already, you can skip over to the next page to find out who we all are.

Best of all, and the thing I've been discovering most, is that God has a gang, too – a huge, enormous gang! And what God wants more than anything is for everyone in the whole world to get to know Him so that they can all be a part of it. A part of His family. Believe me, it SO doesn't get any better than belonging to God.

I should know. I'm one of God's Gang.
See ya!

HI! WE'RE THE TOPZ GANG

– Topz because we all live at the 'top' of something …
either in houses at the top of the hill, at the top of the
flats by the park, even sleeping in a top bunk counts!
We are all Christians, and we go to Holly Hill School.

We love Jesus, and try to work out our faith in God
in everything we do – at home, at school and with our
friends. That even means trying to show God's love to
the Dixons Gang who tend to be bullies, and can be a
real pain!

If you'd like to know more about us, visit our website
at **www.cwr.org.uk/topz** You can read all about us,
and how you can get to know and understand the Bible
more by reading our 'Topz' notes, which are great fun,
and written every two months just for you!

6 JULY — THURSDAY

Not meaning to pick holes or anything, but why did God invent girls? It's not as if they do anything useful or even remotely interesting. A bit like slugs. I mean, what are slugs for other than being disgusting and slimy and winding Mum up by eating all her petunias? I suppose hedgehogs enjoy tucking into a slug snack, but that's about it. You can't even say that for girls. I don't imagine there's a hedgehog on the planet brave enough to tackle munching its way through a whole girl for breakfast. Although apparently they do like cat food.

Anyway, in between being a Sunday Club leader, Louise helps run the open air pool behind the town hall, and she was looking for volunteers to do a bit of a clean-up – changing rooms and stuff – before the big swim gala on Saturday. Topz all said they could go after school today so obviously I said I'd go too because that's the sort of helpful Topzy I am. And even though I had a new Playstation game I couldn't wait to give a go, I was sensationally helpful down at the pool. In fact, nobody could have been more helpful than I was. I was more helpful than the most helpful helping-type person who ever went around helping people who needed helping.

OK, so I didn't do any of the actual changing room cleaning, but I personally think that sometimes you can have too many people cleaning changing rooms and not enough doing the more clever sort of arty stuff, like painting the banner telling everyone what time the gala is on.

Not only that, but the banner I painted was brilliant. Even Benny said it was brilliant, and when Benny says something's brilliant you can be pretty sure that it is because Benny knows things like that. Louise gave me the choice of black or blue paint, so I chose the blue (to be like the water in the pool obviously), then I did my best swirly-type letters and put:

SWIMING GALA THIS SATURDAY 2.00PM BE THERE!!

I mean, boogy-woogily perfect, or what? I was dead happy.

Then Sarah had to go and say, 'You've spelt "SWIMING" all wrong. It's supposed to have another M.'

So, of course, Josie had to add, 'That's true, actually. There should be another M.'

Huh! I mean, stick together, why don't you?

Like I say, girls and slugs. Really. What <u>are</u> they for?

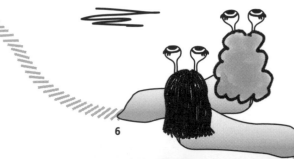

7.30pm

Sarah just ate supper with her back to me.

Mum said, 'I thought twins were supposed to be the best of friends – always there for each other, completely inseparable. What happened to you two?'

Sarah said, 'Nothing's happened to me.'

I said, 'Everything would have been fine if I'd had a twin brother.'

Sarah said, 'Well, everything would have been even more fine if I'd had a twin sister.'

'How d'you work that out?' I said. 'Girls are such rubbish.'

'Is it possible,' Mum interrupted, 'to have just ONE day out of a whole year when you two don't fall out?'

Sarah glanced at me over her shoulder. I glanced at her back. Then –

 we said.

☆ Me and God ☆

Lord God, I know I get angry a lot, but it's not my fault. If Sarah didn't make me angry, there'd be nothing to be angry about. So that means it's Sarah's fault, doesn't it? And if it's Sarah's fault it can't be mine. Full stop. End of the line. No doubt about it. And I've got to ask – why did You make twin sisters so IRRITATING??

7 JULY – FRIDAY

I was really looking forward to youth club tonight. There was Mr Mallory bibble-babbling drearily on in school about times tables, and how anyone who is anyone has learnt them all by the time they're about one year old because they know that times tables are the key to the mathematical universe. And there was me thinking, I DON'T CARE. Six times six can be whatever it wants, I'm just really glad it's Friday so I can go to youth club.

Then, when I got to youth club, all everyone was bibble-babbling on about was the gala at the pool tomorrow (which, by the way, I'm not doing because Sarah's doing it and the last thing I want to do is anything else with Sarah).

I said to Benny, 'Hey, Benny-Bens. D'you fancy coming down the park instead of going to the gala tomorrow?'

He said, 'Nah, I want to swim. You should come along.'

I said to Danny, 'Hey, Danny-Dans. D'you fancy coming down the park instead of going to the gala tomorrow?'

He said, 'Nah, sorry. Mum and Dad are coming to watch me dive.'

Dave wasn't up for it either, which just left Josie and Paul, and there's no way I was asking Josie (girls and slugs, girls and slugs).

Paul said, 'I suppose I could come to the park. It's not as if I'm likely to win any trophies at the pool. Unless it's for who can sink the quickest. What are you planning to get up to?'

'Dunno,' I said. 'We could … kick a ball about.'

'I suppose,' said Paul. 'It's just we can do that any day.'

'Well, we could … hang around on the swings, then. We could play that secret agent game on them where we pretend we're in the space ship being chased by alien spies from alien spy land.'

'We could, it's just –'

I could tell he was losing interest so I jumped in with, 'I know! You could help me test-fly my new kite.' (Technically it's actually Sarah's new kite, but she'll never know if I borrow it because she'll be at the pool.)

'Yeah,' nodded Paul doubtfully. 'Only, what if there's no wind?'

There's no pleasing some people. They find a problem with everything. Fine, I thought. You all push off to your boring old 'swimming with two m's' gala. See if I care. After all, it only takes one person to fly a kite whether there's wind or not. And that's me. One person. An on-my-owner. A-lone.

Yeah. I was really looking forward to youth club. Don't know why I bothered to go now.

me

on my own

8 JULY – SATURDAY

Just had breakfast. Sarah sat with her back to me – again.

Mum said, 'How long's this going to last?'

Sarah said, 'How long's a traffic jam?'

I said, 'Trust a girl to mention jam.'

Dad said, 'Jam? Yes, please. I'll have some with my peanut butter.'

11.00am

Mum says if we can't be nice to each other then can we at least stay in different rooms so that she doesn't have to put up with all the sniping.

I said, 'Fine by me. I've got important stuff to do anyway.'

Sarah said, 'Oh, yeah, like what? The only "important" thing you ever do is take Gruff for a walk, and that's because Gruff's important, not because you are.'

'Shows what you know,' I said. 'Actually I'm entering the competition to design a cover for the new school information pack, so I've got to get it done this weekend to be in time to hand it in.'

'Is that all?' said Sarah. 'Josie and I did that <u>ages</u> ago, and I bet our design is lots better than anything you'll be able to come up with.'

'Bet it's not,' I said.

'Bet it is,' Sarah answered.

'Not!'

'Is!'

'Enough!' shouted Mum. 'Different rooms! Now!'

So here I am, in my bedroom, on my own. Good. (I'm not closing the door, though. Mum didn't say, 'Different rooms and close the doors' – so I'm not closing it.)

11.05am

Wish I'd seen Sarah and Josie's cover design. It's harder to beat something you haven't seen. I <u>will</u> beat it, though. I'll sit here until I come up with the best cover idea in the history of best cover ideas. Today. This morning, even, if it's the last thing I do (which it won't be, obviously. I've got lots more to do than this). One thing's for sure – Josie and Sarah's cover is bound to be all airy-fairy girly-whirly, which will definitely NOT look good on the front of the Holly Hill School info pack. Anyone with half a brain will be able to work that out as soon as they see it. Even teachers like Mr Mallory. <u>My</u> cover, on the other hand, is going to be so amazingly, stonkingly stonking, there won't be another competition entry in the whole school to match its stonkingness.

11.10am
I think I'll start my design in red. Red's good. Girls would never think to start in red.

11.15am
Going well so far. I'm discovering hidden designer depths.

11.20am
Wow, I'm loving this! Really, really!

11.25am
Nope. Bored now. Is it lunchtime, yet?

boring

After lunch-munch

Mum said Sarah and I could both have lunch together in the kitchen provided we sat and faced each other and didn't say anything that wasn't kind and polite. I mean, come on, how hard do lunchtimes have to be? In the end, we didn't say anything at all, which Mum reckoned was an improvement. She's gone with Sarah to the 'swimming with two m's' gala now and Dad's busy on the computer. Wicked. Peace in my own house. No one to bother me. **Zippety-doo-dah.**

1.25pm

Yup. Being on my own is great. Just me, me and me. Couldn't be better.

1.30pm

You see, the trouble with being a twin is it's harder to feel like it's just you because there's always someone else. And in my case, that someone else is Sarah. Which is a <u>lot</u> harder than being twins with someone like Benny, for instance, because that would actually be quite a laugh.

1.35pm

You see, sometimes all I want to be is just ME.

1.40pm

It's dead quiet when Sarah's not here. Even Gruff's asleep.

1.50pm

I said, 'Dad, are you busy?'
He said, 'Afraid I am rather, yes.'

I said, 'I suppose you don't fancy a bit of cricket down the park?'

'Not this afternoon, no,' he said. 'I'm sorry if you're bored, but you should have gone to the gala.'

I shouldn't, actually. And anyway, I'm not bored.

2.00pm
Back to my cover design. It's going to be perfect this time, I can feel it.

2.10pm
I don't know whose idea it was to have a stupid competition to design a stupid cover for the stupid school stupid information pack, but it was a stupid one.

2.15pm
That's it, I'm out of here. I'm taking Gruff for a walk in the park. Just because the Topzies wanted to go swim gala-ing without me, that's no reason why my Saturday afternoon should be rubbish. Besides which I'm having a stonking time on my own. And Paul has made a really HUGE mistake not coming to the park with me because I might just maybe do a bit of kite flying. I know it's Sarah's kite that she bought with her own 'hard-saved pocket money', as she keeps on telling me every time I ask her if I can have a go, but it's not as if she's ever going to use it. She's had it for two weeks already and it just sits in the bottom of her cupboard. Honestly, she hasn't taken it out once – except maybe to tell it how beautiful it is and how much she 'really, really loves it', which is what she was doing the other day when I

walked into her room without knocking. I'm sorry but how sad is that (girls and slugs, girls and slugs)! I think she just bought it because it's shaped like a butterfly so it looks pretty.

In any case, she won't know if I take it or not. She's too busy swim gala-ing. I can go down the park, give it a fly for half an hour, then put it back in her cupboard before she's even out of the pool. Absolute genius idea. I am so good on my own.

Just one small problem. How am I going to sneak a kite past Dad?

Back home – my room (with the door shut)

Big trouble. **Big, BIG** trouble.

Help me.

Oh no, oh no, oh no.

Please help me.

!!!

It isn't my fault. It really isn't my fault.

That's right, actually, it really ISN'T my fault. It's everyone else's.

First of all it's Sarah's fault for being mean about my banner, because otherwise I would have gone to the pool and not down the park at all.

Second it's the Topzies' fault for going to the gala when they could have come down the park with me.

Third it's Dad's fault for not noticing I was trying to get out of the house with Sarah's kite.

Fourth – Dixons. They're the ones who did it.

???

I'm right, though, aren't I? It's their fault, all of them. It can't possibly be mine … except … I took the kite.

4.00pm

Sarah and Mum will be back soon. I'm just going to stay in my room. They'll only be talking about the gala anyway, and I'm not really interested. Actually, I feel a bit sick. If Mum asks me to come downstairs, I'll say, no, I'm not feeling well. Because I'm not. Not at all.

If only I hadn't taken that kite.

I didn't take it to be nasty to Sarah, that wasn't it at all. All I wanted to do was fly it. I knew she'd never let me borrow it, which is really and truly pretty mean when you think about it, and, OK, so it's not that windy today, but I reckoned I could just run up and down on the grass and it would sort of zoom out behind me. In a quiet, whooshy way, of course, because it's not the sort of kite to make a lot of loud zooming noises.

So I went into Sarah's bedroom, sneaked it out of her cupboard, crept downstairs so Dad wouldn't hear and put it outside the back door. Then I put Gruff on his lead, told Dad we were going down to the park, picked up the kite on our way out, and Dad never even knew I had it. It should have been perfect. I mean, it was a really clever plan. The sort of clever plan I can easily come up with when I'm on my own and not being hassled by everyone else.

To start with, it was all so great being just me and Gruff at the park – much better than going to some dippy old gala. I ran up and down between the two football goals with Gruff chasing after me, running his little legs off. He was doing his yappy bark thing and the butterfly kite was bouncing up and down in the air making zig zags and swooping and diving. It didn't go very high because, like I say, there wasn't much wind, but it stayed up pretty well. There was one fairly spectacular crash-landing and I thought, whoops – that wasn't meant to happen.

Only it wasn't the crash that broke it.

It was Dixons.

I never even saw them. They came

out of nowhere. I suppose they must have been hiding in the trees at the bottom end of the park because I'd just reached the goalpost when suddenly they were all around me. I dropped the kite and grabbed Gruff. I thought they were going to try and nab him. But they weren't interested in Gruff. Not this time.

'What's all this, then?' said Clyde, the ginger one. 'Has John gone and got himself a kite?'

'Cool,' said Ricky (thin one, long, straight hair). 'I always wanted a kite.'

'Not much of a kite, though, is it?' sneered the other one, Kevin. 'Who wants a kite shaped like a butterfly?'

'Me!' said Ricky. 'I don't care what it's shaped like. Like I say, I always wanted a kite.' Then he bent down and picked it up.

'N – no,' I managed to gulp. 'You can't have it. It's not mine, I'm just borrowing it.'

Ricky turned and looked straight at me.

'Is that right?' he said. 'Well, guess what? Now I'm just borrowing it.'

I looked round at them. All three of them. They seemed so much bigger than me – and Ricky's hair is really greasy when you see him close up, and bits of his fringe were falling into his eyes.

'Look, I'm sorry and everything,' I mumbled, 'but you can't have it. I've got to take it home.'

'And what happens if you don't?' said Kevin. 'Will you get into trouble?'

'Yeah,' I nodded. 'Yeah, I will.'

'Aww!' smirked Clyde. 'What a shame.'

'So, will you give it back then?' I asked. I don't know why because I knew they weren't going to.

'Oooh, let's think about that for a minute,' said Ricky, scratching his chin. 'No!'

Then he turned and went to run off with the kite, but I knew I couldn't let him, so I made a grab for it. Only when I'd got my fingers tight round the frame, Ricky yanked it towards him. He yanked it dead hard. And that's when it snapped. Broke clean through. I looked down and there was one butterfly wing just flapping about. Wrecked.

'Oops,' said Ricky, right in my face. 'Now look what you've done.'

'Yeah,' grinned Clyde. 'Looks like you're going to be in trouble after all.'

Suddenly Ricky pulled the whole thing out of my hand and dropped it on the grass.

'You know what, Kev?' he said. 'I think you're right. A butterfly is a pretty stupid shape for a kite.'

Then he stamped on it. Sarah's kite that she'd bought with her hard-saved pocket money. Sarah's kite that she loved. Sarah's beautiful butterfly. He just stamped on it with his dirty, brown boot, and they all ran off, laughing.

As soon as they were out of sight, I put Gruff down and clipped his lead back on. It wasn't that easy, actually. My hands were shaking, I was so scared. But of all the things I imagined Dixons might do, I never thought it'd be that. I never thought they'd be that horrible. I mean it wasn't even <u>my</u> kite they were breaking.

I picked it up but I could see there was nothing to be done. I couldn't mend it. I wiped off the mud left by Ricky's boot, but there was nothing else.

It was ruined.

Forever.

And it's all my fault.

9.30pm

Sarah hasn't found her kite, yet. I managed to slide it into her cupboard when I got home from the park without Dad noticing. (He doesn't notice much when he's on the computer.) I even put Sarah's Scrabble game on top of it. There's so much stuff jammed into that cupboard, I thought it might look as though the box had fallen down onto it from one of the shelves and broken the frame when it landed.

Well, I can hardly tell her it was my fault, can I? I can't just say, 'Sorry, it was me, I took your kite.' For one thing everybody would think I was horrible and for another, Sarah would hate me for the rest of my life and, to be honest, whether she finds out or not, I think <u>I'm</u> going to hate me for the rest of my life.

I don't want to feel like this. I didn't mean for it to get broken. I mean, it's just a silly kite. Why does it have to FEEL LIKE THIS?

☆ Me and God ☆

I don't know what to do, Lord. I don't know how to make this knot in my tummy go away. It's just sitting there all hard and sore. I'm not going to tell Sarah what I've done. I can't. I mean, as long as she doesn't find out, in the end this feeling will go away, won't it, because no one will know I've done anything wrong so it'll be like it never happened? Besides, she's being nice now. When I said I was going to bed she was all, 'Please don't be sulky about the gala banner any more. Anyone can make a spelling mistake.' Not anyone can get your kite broken, though, I thought. That takes someone really mean. Really selfish. Really stupid. Someone like me. I'm sorry I took it, Lord. I wish today had never happened.

9 JULY — SUNDAY

I was dreaming that Sarah had given me a goldfish for my birthday – which was mega odd because I've never thought about keeping goldfish and it's nowhere near my birthday – when she woke me up, screaming. Well, I suppose it wasn't really a scream. More like a loud moan.

I heard Mum rush into her bedroom saying, 'What's the matter, sweetheart, are you all right?'

I didn't need to hear what Sarah said, though. And I didn't need anyone to tell me what was wrong. I knew Sarah's moan meant she'd found her kite.

She cried all the way through breakfast.

Dad said, 'Come on, Sarah, it's not worth getting this upset. It's only a kite after all. You can get another one.'

'But I don't want another one,' she sobbed, jabbing at her Frosties with her spoon as if it was all their fault. 'I loved <u>that</u> one. I saved up for it and everything. It's special. It's my butterfly.'

'Well, maybe Dad can mend it,' Mum suggested.

'I can have a look,' said Dad, 'but I don't know. I'm not the world's best at mending things.'

'Even if it's mended, it won't be the same,' Sarah coughed. 'It was perfect and now it's not.'

'Well, one thing's for sure,' continued Mum, 'before anything else goes in that cupboard, we need to clear it out. It's a tip in there. I'm not surprised something's got broken.'

I couldn't sit there any longer.

I had to get out of the kitchen.

'Where are you off to?' Dad asked.

'Just upstairs,' I mumbled.

'What's up, then?' he said. 'You're very quiet.'

'No, I'm not,' I answered.

Yes, I am, actually. And anyone would be quiet if they'd done what I'd done.

⭐ Me and God ⭐

I got away with it, Lord God. They think it was the Scrabble box. They think a stupid game of Scrabble fell on Sarah's kite and that's what broke it. No one's got any idea it had anything to do with me. Isn't that cool? No one's ever going to find out and Sarah doesn't have to hate me. Wicked ... So how come I still feel so bad?

In bed

I'm in big trouble. Huge trouble. Mega enormous trouble. So much trouble I think I'm going to stay in my bedroom for the rest of my life.

THEY KNOW ...

10 JULY — MONDAY

Weird how stuff happens. It's all fine and then suddenly – it's just not. You don't even mean it to go bad, but somehow it does and there's nothing you can do about it.

I said that to Dad and he went, 'What you shouldn't have done is take Sarah's kite. Things wouldn't have gone bad if you hadn't done the wrong thing in the first place.'

It was at Sunday Club where it all came out. It would have been pretty obvious even to someone with their head down a hole that Sarah had been bawling her eyes out, so, of course, Louise had to ask her what the matter was and Sarah had to tell her.

Paul happened to be getting the pens out of the cupboard at the time and was listening to every word.

'It's surprising how heavy a Scrabble box is,' I heard him say. 'I had one fall on my head once when I was looking for my 'How To Take Care Of Your Microscope' book. I never found it either, which is a real shame because it's a REALLY good book. What were we talking about? Oh, yeah. Sorry about your kite, but don't be upset. I'm sure John will let you borrow his.'

The hard lump in my stomach shot up into my throat.

'He probably would if he could but John doesn't have a kite,' Sarah snivelled.

I tried to swallow the lump down but it wouldn't move.

'Yes, he does,' said Paul. 'He asked me to fly it with him down the park instead of going to the gala yesterday, but I sort of wanted to go to the gala so I said no.'

I'm not sure what happened next. I know Sarah was suddenly looking at me as if I was some sort of ugly, dribbly monster. She got it quick as a flash – almost, that is: she'd gone to the gala; I'd snatched her kite; I'd smashed it up in the park; and I'd stuffed it back in her cupboard under the Scrabble box to make it look as though it had got broken accidentally.

Obviously the part Sarah didn't get was that I didn't break her kite on purpose and, actually, it wasn't me who broke it at all. But seeing the expression on her face, somehow I didn't think she was going to be very interested in hearing about that.

She pushed past me when it was time to go home and all she said was,

'Butterfly killer.'

After breakfast

I can't believe I'm actually glad it's school today. It's worse than that, though. I'm even feeling happy I'm going to be shut up in the same room with Mr Mallory for hours. Guess why? It means I don't have to worry about seeing Sarah. I used to think Sarah's class with

Mrs Parker sounded heaps more fun than mine. I even asked Mrs Parker once if I could swap forms because she did much more interesting things than Mr Mallory, like team quizzes and messy stuff and pretending to be crocodiles in swamps, but she said no and, for my information, Mr Mallory had some very interesting things up his sleeve. I've no idea what she was talking about because anyone with eyes in their brains can see that Mr Mallory and interesting things just don't go together, but I'm glad she said no now. I wouldn't go in Sarah's class if you paid me. Living in the same house is going to be enough of a problem. I don't want to have to see her again. Not ever. It just makes me feel SO BAD knowing that every time she looks at me she's thinking, butterfly killer. As if I don't feel bad enough already.

So, Mr Mallory's great. School's great. I might even ask if I can move in permanently. I could have my bed in a corner of the classroom and in the daytime we could cover it up with a big plastic sheet and use it as a craft table. And food wouldn't be a problem. I could live on everyone else's leftover packed lunches. There's always the odd bit of sandwich or half a yoghurt hanging around in the cloakroom at the end of the day. I trod in a bit of Swiss roll once – which Benny said was a shame because it was one of the chocolate ones and he could have eaten it.

And then there's the other thing. I've made up my mind. I'm not a twin any more. It's too much trouble. I'm just John. On my own. Me. And that's it, really.

4.30pm: My den

OK, so it's my bedroom, but from now on it's my den – where I can hang out in private. Just me, right away from prying, butterfly killer eyes. Even Mum's doing it now – giving me the look. I think I'll have to invent a secret knock and only specially selected people who knock on my door with the secret knock (ie probably no one) will be allowed in.

John's Den
KEEP OUT
PRIVATE
STRICTLY NO ADMITANCE
(except with secret knock!
Which only I know!!!)

At lunchtime, so I could avoid Sarah outside, I asked Mr Mallory if I could stay indoors and tidy the bookshelves.

He said, 'Wonder of wonders, John – do my ears deceive me or are you actually offering to be helpful? You must have been bitten by a good deed fairy in the night.'

'Does that mean I can?' I asked hopefully.

'It means you must be up to something so, no,' he said.

What is it with teachers? They moan at you for not being helpful and then, when you offer to be helpful, they don't want your help. Loony-macarooni, or what?

After lunch I sat with Dave round the back of the changing huts and told him what had really happened in the park on Saturday. Sarah and Josie were out on the field, so I wasn't going to hang around there. Besides, I had to tell someone, and whenever I've got something to tell, I usually tell it to Dave.

Dave said, 'You really ought to tell your mum and dad about the Dixons. They're the reason the kite got broken.'

'It's not important how it happened,' I said. 'It's like Dad says, I shouldn't have taken it in the first place.'

'OK, there is that, I suppose,' he shrugged, 'but it still wasn't your fault what happened. Anyway, we all do things wrong. I once dropped Dad's electric razor down the toilet when I was practising a juggling trick, and I shouldn't even have been using it to practise a juggling trick. Certainly not near the toilet. The whizzy round bits only worked at half-speed afterwards, which meant Dad's cheeks were still half-bristly after he'd shaved. But I didn't do it on purpose and he knows that.'

'You mean, your dad still used his electric razor after it'd been down the toilet?' I said.

'I know,' Dave nodded, 'but Dad hates wasting things. The only reason he bought a new one in the end is because Mum ran away screaming every time he went to kiss her goodbye when he went to work in the mornings.'

'Right,' I said. 'Anyway, at least you didn't get looked at with electric razor killer eyes. I know I took the kite when I shouldn't have, but I didn't mean for it to get broken. And that's what nobody seems to understand.'

'Which is why you've got to tell them about the Dixons,' said Dave.

I shook my head. 'There's no point. They'll just think I'm making it up.'

In bed

I reckon Sarah must have spent all day thinking, *how can I make this as bad as possible for John? I know! I won't sit with my back to him while we're eating, I'll sit right in front of him and STARE at him the whole time with my butterfly killer eyes. That'll fix him.*

It did, too. It fixed me well and truly. I couldn't stick it.

I blurted out, 'Look, I've said I'm sorry I took your kite. I've said I never meant for it to end up getting broken. I'm even saving up my pocket money so I can buy you a new one. I don't know what else to do. Why can't you just LEAVE ME ALONE?!'

I stormed off back to my den and slammed the door. Everything downstairs was dead quiet for a while. Then I heard a knock. I hadn't shown anyone my secret knock, so it was just a normal sort of knock, but I was pretty sure it was Dad.

Only it wasn't. It was Dave.

'Is it safe to come in?' he asked.

'What are you doing here?' I said. 'You knock just like Dad.'

'Your dad was out the front and said to go on up. Although he did say to watch myself because you were in a bit of a mood.'

'You see?' I groaned. 'Why is no one ever on my side?'

'That's a bit harsh,' Dave said. 'In case you haven't noticed, I'm on your side. Why else would I be here when I could be changing the brakes on my bike? Anyway, what are you doing in bed? It's only quarter past seven.'

'It's <u>my</u> den,' I answered. 'If I want to go to bed, I'll go to bed.'

'Fair enough, I suppose. So, I take it from the "bit of a mood" comment that you haven't told them yet.'

'Of course I haven't told them,' I snapped, 'and I'm not going to either. Besides, why do you care so much? It's not your problem.'

'Because I'm you're mate, dimbo,' Dave said.

That's it, you see, that's why I always tell Dave stuff. Because Dave's my mate.

'The thing is, I was praying for you,' he went on, 'and I'm sure God wants me to help you sort this out. I think we should go and tell everyone what happened to Sarah's kite in the park right now.'

Sometimes you know you can argue till your hair falls out but in the end it's pointless. So I didn't even bother to try and we did what Dave said. We told them. At least Dave told them. I said I couldn't, I really couldn't, so he just went and talked to Mum and Dad and Sarah on his own. Imagine that. He did that for me. Dave's more than a mate. He's a super-mate.

Next thing I knew, there was another knock on my door.

I said, 'Yeah, Dave, what happened?'

Only it wasn't Dave. It was Dad.

He said, 'What are you doing in bed?'

I said, 'It's <u>my</u> den. If I want to go to bed, I'll go to bed.'

'It looks as if you're hiding to me,' Dad smiled. Then he sat down beside me and said, 'Why didn't you tell us about the Dixons?'

'There wasn't any point,' I said. 'You wouldn't have believed me. You'd have thought I was making it up so I didn't get into trouble.'

'That's not true,' said Dad.

'Isn't it?' I said.

'No,' he said. 'You'd still have got in trouble because you shouldn't have taken Sarah's kite.'

'Thanks,' I said.

'And the other reason it's not true is that I know you and I know you wouldn't lie about something like that. You can be a bit of a grump and you certainly need to try and keep that temper of yours under control, but you're not a liar. And I actually think the world of you.'

'Really?' I said.

'Really,' he answered. 'But those Dixons, now that's another story. They need someone to have a firm word or two with them, so I'll pop over their way later.'

'No.' I shook my head. 'No, don't, Dad.'

'They need to be told, John,' Dad said. 'They need to know you can't go around breaking other people's things.'

'But they didn't break it,' I sighed, 'at least not on purpose. It got broken when I tried to get it back. Anyway, like you say, it's my fault. If I hadn't taken it, it wouldn't have happened.'

That's when there was a knock on my door <u>again</u>.

'It's OK, Mum, you can come in,' I said.

Only it wasn't Mum. It was Sarah. I tell you what, this knocking business can be dead confusing.

Sarah said, 'What are you doing in bed?'

Like I say, dead confusing. I was sure I'd had that conversation before.

'Anyway,' she went on, 'just wanted to say sorry I've been so nasty. You're not a butterfly killer at all. I should have known really. I should have known you could never do something so horrible.'

'Cool,' I said. 'Thanks.'

'Don't get me wrong,' she burbled on, 'I mean, you're a total barn pot and you're really annoying and sometimes you drive me up the absolute wall, round the bend and up a mountain. But you're not horrible.'

OK. I think.

11 JULY — TUESDAY

Spent lunchtime with Dave round the back of the changing huts. Not because I was hiding from anyone but because sometimes you need to say stuff to someone without anyone like, say, Danny bounding up and going, 'How about a goalie contest?' or Benny leaping about and whooping, 'Were those spicy bean burgers hot or what?'

Dave said, 'So, you all sorted now, then?'

I said, 'Yeah. Thanks to you.'

'Not thanks to me,' he said. 'It's thanks to God. He's the One who told me to help you out. And when you get the nudge like that, you've just got to do something.'

Dave's actually pretty incredible. I mean, I know he's

been a Christian longer than I have but I guess he must be stonkingly brave to hear God telling him to do something and then just get up and go and do it. He says this time it wasn't that big a deal because talking to Mum and Dad wasn't too hard for him, but it's not always like that. Sometimes, he says, God has to tell Him to do things lots of times before He does anything at all, and even then He tries to find a million excuses for not bothering. A bit like Jonah in the Bible. God told Jonah to go to a city called Nineveh and tell the people there to stop doing wrong things and obey Him. But Jonah didn't want to, so he ran away in completely the opposite direction. Only you can't run away from God, so in the end he had to do what God wanted anyway. And if he'd only done it in the first place, he could have saved himself being nearly drowned and swallowed by a big fish.

To Nineveh

Not Nineveh

Paul once said he wouldn't mind being swallowed by a big fish for a few days.

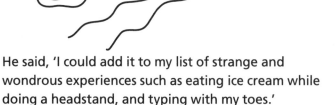

BURP

He said, 'I could add it to my list of strange and wondrous experiences such as eating ice cream while doing a headstand, and typing with my toes.'

Josie said, 'Wouldn't the smell of fish stomach bother you?'

Paul said, 'No. I smell anyway.'

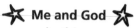 Me and God

Dad says that when we do things wrong, it's not just other people we hurt. It's You as well. I'm sorry I hurt You, Lord God. And I'm sorry I hurt Sarah and made her sad. I don't know what it is sometimes. I just get so angry and it takes me over. When Sarah said I'd made a spelling mistake on that banner, all I wanted to do was get back at her because she made me feel … well … stupid. Stupid and useless. So I thought, I know, I'll go off on my own. I'll show her I don't need anybody and I certainly don't need her. I can have a great time by myself.

Only it wasn't a great time. It was a bad time.

But, the thing is, Lord, You never give up on us when we do the wrong thing, do You? Look at Jonah. He did totally the wrong thing and ended up inside a fish, but You never gave up. You just kept on at Him, until he did what was right and what You wanted Him to do.

Dad says You're not looking for perfect people to be Your friends because people just aren't perfect. They ignore You. They do wrong things, things that make You sad – just like I did when I got angry and took Sarah's kite. Only Dad says You love us anyway. Just as we are. With all our not perfect bits. He says that whatever we do wrong, You still want to forgive us. We just have to come to You and say sorry and try again.

So this is me trying again. Thank You for not giving up on me. Thank You for Mum and Dad and Sarah. Being a twin has its up side too, I suppose. And thank You for my best mate, Dave. Help me always to be ready to help him the way he's helped me.

That's about it, I think. Amen.

13 JULY — THURSDAY

Dave rang before school.

He said, 'Forgot to say. We're having a muffin cook-off at Boys' Brigade later.'

I said, 'You're having a whaty what-off?'

'A muffin cook-off. We're going to see how many muffins we can cook in two hours. Greg says we can bring a friend so d'you want to come?'

I said, 'I'm not very good at cooking.'

Dave said, 'Neither am I. Neither's Benny, but he's coming with Paul. In fact Benny wanted to change it to how many muffins you can <u>eat</u> in two hours, but Greg said that was missing the point because he wants to sell them at youth club tomorrow to raise money for the new homeless shelter. What d'you think?'

'Sounds cool,' I said.

Sarah said, 'What does?'

When I told her she went, 'Eeew. Who'd want to eat muffins cooked by a load of boys?'

Eeew!

Boys!

Zippety zonkas!

I breezed passed her and whispered, 'Girls and slugs, girls and slugs.'

'Pardon?' said Sarah.

'Nothing.'

It's great having things back to normal.

33

15 JULY — SATURDAY

There are different shades of normal. That's what Sarah sometimes says when she's trying to be all wise and knowing. She reckons there's ordinary normal, which can be anything from light grey to leaf green; there's out-of-the-ordinary normal, which can be sky blue to bright red; there's whizzy-dizzy normal which is jazzy orange with purple spots. Then there are other types of normal, good and bad, when it's hard to think of a colour that fits.

I used to think all this meant Sarah was even weirder than I reckoned she was, but today I understand. She's right. There <u>are</u> different shades of normal. The last couple of days have been SO orange and SO purply-spotty. Stonking in other words.

Then today happened and suddenly I don't know what colour anything is. The only one in my head isn't very nice. It's a sort of dark bluey-black. Like a bruise.

My den

I got back from walking Gruff and Sarah said, 'Are you OK? You look as if you've just been chased by a monster.'

Mum said, 'Yes, you do actually, John. What's the matter? Has something happened?'

I said, 'No. I'm just tired.'

'Must be all that cooking for Boys' Brigade,' Mum smiled.

'Must be,' I answered.

34

The muffin cook-off at Boys' Brigade was brilliant. So was youth club. We sold every single cake yesterday and raised £25. Wicked start to the weekend, I thought. This is going to be a good one.

But that was before this afternoon. That was before I took Gruff out for a walk up towards the shopping centre instead of going to the park like I usually do. That was before I got chased by a monster.

A monster called the Dixons.

If I'd known they were going to be hanging around at the top of the alley, I'd never have gone that way. It's just that Gruff was having a snifty. He has days like that when all he seems to want to do is sniff, and he'd been sniffle-snaffling ever since we left home, which is mostly why we didn't go to the park. Anyway, we got to the end of the alley and whatever smell he was tracking led right up it, so he just yanked me off round the corner. Gruff gets very excited about smells. Sometimes it's easiest just to let his nose lead the way. It's just that today, that's the last thing I should have done – because Gruff's nose led us crash bang flollop into trouble.

Ricky saw us first.

'Look who it is,' he said.

'Oh, yeah,' grinned Kevin. 'Look, Clyde, it's Kite Boy and his little, furry friend.'

'All right, Kite Boy?' said Clyde. 'Hope you didn't get in too much trouble last weekend.'

They all started laughing. Gruff was sniffing round a scrunched up Burger King bag. I tried to pull him away so that we could just scoot off in the other direction but, like I say, Gruff's nose can be as stubborn as Sarah, so that was the end of the quick getaway plan. The Dixons shuffled a bit closer.

'Aww,' whined Ricky. 'Aren't you talking to us any more?'

I didn't know what to do. I thought, 'if I run off now, they'll easily catch me before I get to the end. Maybe I should just try and talk to them normally, as if they're Topzies, and then they'll leave me alone. I mean, how hard can it be?'

'Of course, I'm talking to you,' I managed to mumble. 'Why wouldn't I be? So … what are you up to, then?'

I should have known better. Whatever I'd said would have been wrong. They all stopped laughing.

'Why?' snapped Clyde. 'What's it to you?'

'N-nothing,' I began. 'Anyway, I've got to go now.'

'Where?' Kevin demanded.

I wanted to say, 'Why? What's it to you?' Only, of course, I didn't. I didn't say anything.

'I know where he's going,' said Ricky, peering at me through his greasy fringe. I don't reckon he ever washes his hair. 'He's going to find all his little Topzy mates so they can sit down together and have a lovely, cosy chat with God.'

'Oh, yeah,' said Clyde. 'Did you remember to tell

Him you're sorry for being naughty and smashing up someone else's kite? Tut tut.'

'Of course he remembered,' said Kevin, 'because John's a little goody-goody, aren't you, John? A boring, little goody-goody.'

He spat the last bit out and shoved his face at me. I must have looked all scared and pathetic or something because they suddenly all burst out laughing again.

That's when I ran. I turned and belted out of the alley dragging Gruff along behind me. If they caught me, they caught me. All I knew was I had to get out of there.

As I got to the corner they were still howling with laughter and I heard one of them yell, 'Hey, Johnny!

BOO!'

4.30pm
Benny rang.

He said, 'Meeting Danny at the skateboard park in 5 – 4 – 3 – 2 – 1. In other words, going over there now. Wanna come?'

'No,' I said. 'Thanks, though.'

'Oh, go on,' he said. 'I've learnt this new trick. If it goes right it looks totally cool and fantasmagorical, and if it goes wrong I end up on my bottom – which Danny says is hilarious, so either way it's worth a look.'

'Groovy, but no,' I said. 'I'm staying in.'

What else can I do? Everywhere I go I bump into Dixons and they won't leave me alone. Even if Benny and Danny are there, they'll still have a go. So I'm not going skateboarding. I'm not going anywhere. I'm staying in.

Later

Weird Saturday. Weird and wonky. Bluey-black. Like last week, now I come to think of it. I felt like a sad little loser back then. Why do I have to feel like that all over again? It's not fair. Being friends with God should be a good thing. Why do the Dixons have to turn it into something bad?

☆ Me and God ★

Why? **Why?**

Why did you let it happen, Lord? Why did you let the Dixons pick on me because I'm Your friend? That's why they hate all us Topz. Because we love You and try to live the way You want us to. It's not easy, though. I sometimes think that maybe if I wasn't a Christian and I ignored You like they do, everything would be OK with them. They'd leave me alone because they wouldn't think I was any different from the way <u>they</u> are. Only I know You. I know how much You've done for me. You're my best friend so I <u>can't</u> ignore You. I don't even <u>want </u>to ignore You. What I <u>do</u> want is to understand why You let it happen. Why did I have to end up feeling so … bruised?

why? **Why**

Why? **Why?** **Why?**

In bed

Sarah walked into my den to borrow my atlas.

She said, 'Are you in bed again? It's getting earlier and earlier.'

I said, 'Don't you ever knock?'

She said, 'I'll start knocking on your door when you start knocking on mine.'

'Whatever,' I sighed.

'Anyway, like I was saying,' she said, 'are you in bed again?'

'Well, duh,' I said from my lying-in-bed position.

'What I mean is,' she yabbered on, raising her eyes like Mum does when she's said no about fourteen times and you're still asking her the same question, 'what are you doing there? If you spend much more time lying in bed under your duvet, you'll turn into a huge, flobby, marshmallow-looking blob. Then you'll be all sad and lonely with no one to talk to because no one will recognise you any more, not even Mum and Dad.'

Funny she should say that, really, because I don't think I could feel much more sad and lonely than I do at the moment. Although being flobby and marshmallow-looking would probably make it even worse.

I shrugged and said, 'Whatever,' again.

39

She stopped trying to find the atlas then and turned and looked at me.

'Aren't you even going to argue?' she asked.

'What's the point?' I answered.

'The point is you usually argue with everything I say,' she answered. 'Are you OK?'

'I've been wondering something, that's all,' I said. 'How do you feel when people call you names for being a Christian?'

'Has someone been calling you names for being a Christian?' Sarah said. 'Who?'

'No one,' I said. I didn't want to talk about that bit. 'I just wondered how it made you feel.'

'Don't really know,' she shrugged. 'Charlotte Miller sometimes says nasty things at school, but Charlotte Miller says nasty things to lots of people, so I just try not to take any notice.'

'But when she's saying nasty things,' I went on, 'don't you ever think, why doesn't God stop her? After all, He's your friend. Why does He let things like that happen?'

'Mum always says that being friends with God doesn't mean that bad things are never going to happen to us. But what it does mean is that, whatever goes on day by day, the good things and the bad things, He'll always stay with us, helping us through. He'll be there no matter what.' Sarah paused. 'Are you sure no one's been calling you names?'

'Quite sure,' I nodded.

'In that case,' she said, 'I've got to tell you that you must have the messiest bookcase I have ever had to try and find an atlas in.

How do know where –'

She broke off suddenly. Then, 'Eeew,' she murmured. Slowly, using only the very, very tips of her fingers, from in between two books she pulled out something small and black with what looked a lot like Gruff's hair randomly stuck to it. At least I hope it was Gruff's hair.

'What on earth is that?' I asked.

'I'm not sure,' Sarah said, 'but I think it might once have been a Liquorice Allsort.'

16 JULY — SUNDAY

At Sunday Club, Paul was dead excited.

He said, 'Dad found an old pram down at the recycling centre and he's going to take the wheels off and help me build a go-kart. Today. This afternoon. D'you want to come round? Danny's coming. And Dave. Benny says he would only his mum's just bought an ice cream maker so he might be a bit busy doing ice cream tasting. So what d'you think? Can you come?'

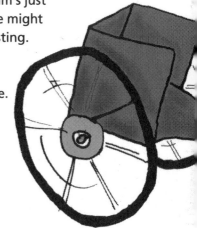

'Sounds wicked,' I said. 'Maybe. You know, I'll see how it goes.'

'How it goes,' Paul jabbered on, 'will be ultra-cool, ultra-smooth on four ultra-fast pram wheels! You've just got to be there.'

I'd like to be there, I really would. It's just that, if you build a go-kart, the first thing you'll want to do is try it out. And where do you go to try it out? The park. And who's probably going to be at the park? Dixons. And who are the last people I want to see today?

Yup, got it in one.

All things considered, I think I'll just stay in my den.

After lunch

Been sitting on the garden wall out the front with Dad. I like sitting on the wall with Dad. We play this game where we each choose a car colour and then have to spot as many of that colour car as we can. First to twenty usually wins, but I said today could we make it first to fifty.

Dad said, 'That's a lot of green cars I've got to spot, but OK.'

To be honest, I wasn't that bothered about the car spotting. I just wanted to sit on the wall with Dad for as long as possible. After all, if I'm sitting on the wall with Dad I can't be doing anything else. Like go-kart building, for instance. I'll just have to say to Paul tomorrow, 'Sorry I didn't come go-kart building. I was sitting on the wall with Dad. He likes it when I sit on the wall with him. It's one of those important things we do together.'

John – pink | Dad – green
 | ༈༈༈ I

I hadn't spotted any pink cars (but then I didn't expect to – the only reason I chose pink was because there more than likely wouldn't be any which meant the game might last a bit longer) and Dad was up to his sixth green one when he said, 'Sarah tells me you've got a new hobby.'

'I don't think so,' I said.

'Oh yeah,' said Dad. 'She says you're working at turning into a marshmallow-looking blob.'

Thanks, Sarah. There may not be much to choose between girls and slugs, but there are days when I reckon a slug would make a far better twin.

'What's that all about, then?' Dad asked. 'These days, I must be honest, I could happily spend a whole Saturday in bed if your mum would let me, but when I was your age it was the last place I wanted to be. I needed to be out there, kicking a ball, riding my bike, jumping in the pond. I had a whole  host of bed-avoiding tricks up my sleeve. Ask your gran. She'll tell you.'

I can't picture Dad jumping in a pond. He doesn't even like getting his feet wet.

He went on, 'So what's with all this going to bed early? Come on, you can tell me. I've got extremely big ears.'

I smiled but I still didn't say anything.

Dad sighed. 'If you don't start talking to me in the next ten seconds, I'm afraid I'm going to have to push you off this wall.'

'OK,' I said. 'I just like going to bed to think, that's all. And what I've been thinking is this. Not that it's remotely to do with me or anything, but, if someone's picking on you for being a Christian ... what should you do?'

'That's an odd thing to be thinking if it's got nothing to do with you,' Dad said, turning to look at me, which I really didn't want him to do in case I gave myself away.

'Not really,' I shrugged. 'I'm always thinking odd things. Bit of an odd things thinker, I suppose. Anyway, watch the road. You just missed a green car.'

'Yes, right, sorry,' said Dad. 'Well, I think that if someone is being picked on for being a Christian, then the most important thing they need to know is that whatever they're going through, Jesus is standing right beside them the whole time and, chances are, He's been through it, too. Jesus came to earth to live as an ordinary human being like you and me. He knows what it's like. I'm sure He must have fallen over and scraped His knees when He was growing up, or felt tired at the end of a hard day's work, or even just wanted a bit of space to lie in bed and be left alone to think. Exactly like you. Not that He probably got a lot of that.'

Mmm, I thought. I know the feeling. Although I've never thought of Jesus falling over and scraping His knees.

'And d'you know what else Jesus knows about?' Dad went on. 'Jesus knows about suffering. People hated Him because He said He was the Son of God. They hated Him because He showed them all the things they were doing wrong. They hated Him so much that they all got together and killed Him. But before they killed Him, they made Him suffer and they made fun of Him and they called Him names. And even through all that, He stuck to the truth and He never let God down.'

He paused a moment then added quietly, 'So you see, John, if someone's picking on you for being a Christian, Jesus knows exactly how it feels. And He will never leave you to deal with it on your own. You've just got to ask Him to help you.'

I noticed Dad was looking at me again, so I turned my face right away and pretended to be searching the road for pink cars.

'You can always talk to me, you know,' he said to the back of my head. 'I'll help you with whatever the trouble is.'

'Thanks,' I said, 'but if there aren't any pink cars, there aren't any pink cars. I think you're definitely going to win.'

7.00pm
Dave came round. Dad and I were still on the wall.

'You've just got to come and try out Paul's go-kart,' he said. 'It is wicked!'

'Yeah?' I said.

'Yeah!' he said. 'What are you waiting for?'

'Fifty pink cars, I think,' Dad said.

Once we'd decided I'd got about as much chance of spotting fifty pink cars going down our road as I had of seeing one flying double-decker bus, I couldn't think of any more excuses. So I ended up in the park. On the go-kart. And Dave was right. It <u>was</u> wicked.

We took turns pushing each other round the outside of the football pitch first of all, which was a mega laugh because none of us could steer to save our lives and we kept ending up in the bushes – especially when Danny was pushing because he pelted us round. But the best bit was whizzing down the slope near the swings. We only had our feet for brakes and if you timed kicking them out wrong, you shot off to the right and ended up nose down in the sand pit! Groovy or what? Fortunately, there was never anyone in the sand at the time. Still, Paul said that if there ever was, we all had to yell, 'Coming THROOOOUGH!'

at the tops of our voices before we crashed because, after all, if we ran into someone we might break the go-kart. Sounds fair to me.

Anyway, it was all going great, and I was quite glad I wasn't still sitting on my wall looking for pink cars, when out of the blue, slap bang doodley-doo, THEY had to go and turn up again. Them. Dixons. Urgh.

I didn't see them to start with so I don't know how long they'd been watching, but I'd just crashed in the sand pit for the I-don't-know-how-manyth time when I heard Ricky shouting, 'Oi, John! You need some driving lessons, mate!'

'Take no notice,' said Dave. 'It's like they've got nothing better to do than hang around annoying people.'

He helped me drag the go-kart out of the sand pit, but suddenly the three Dixons were standing right in front of us.

'Cool kart,' said Clyde. 'Whose is it, Johnny? Or are you "borrowing" it like you do with kites?'

I opened my mouth to answer but Paul stepped forward.

'It's mine, actually,' he said, 'and John can borrow it any time he wants, which is more than any of you can, kite wreckers.' I was quite surprised. I mean, he sounded pretty tough but I could tell he was scared. I wondered whether the Dixons could, too.

'Did you hear that, guys?' said Clyde. 'Paul thinks we're kite wreckers.'

'I don't <u>think</u>,' said Paul. 'I <u>know</u>.'

'Yeah?' snarled Kevin. 'And d'you know what else we are? GO-KART WRECKERS!'

All of a sudden, he lifted his foot, all laced up in a

great big boot, and was about to bring it crashing down on top of the kart when there was a shout from behind us.

'If that go-kart isn't still in one piece by the time I get to it, there's going to be serious trouble!'

We all turned. We all saw him. We were all pretty gob-smacked, especially Paul. It was his dad!

'No worries, Mr Paul's Dad,' Clyde smirked. 'Kev was only goofing about, weren't you, Kev?'

Kev, who was so surprised he was till standing over the kart with his foot dangling in mid-air, almost lost his balance and fell over. He just managed to save himself when Clyde gave him a shove which sent him sprawling face first into the sand pit. I couldn't believe it! None of us could, and we all had to try not to laugh.

'Glad that's sorted, then,' said Paul's dad, 'because I spent a long time putting that go-kart together with the aid of my trusty adjustable screwdriver, and I would <u>not</u> be happy if anything happened to it. Now,' he went on, looking round at us Topzies, 'who's going to give me a push round the football pitch?'

He headed off towards the goalposts and Paul and Danny started to pull the kart along behind him. Dave and I followed on, but Ricky caught hold of my sleeve. It was only for a moment but long enough for him to hiss, 'So you think this is funny, do you? Well, I bet you wouldn't be laughing if you were down here all on your own. Always got to have your goody-goody Gang around, haven't you? I reckon you're too <u>scared</u> to come down here by yourself.'

Dave turned round just as he let me go. He must have seen my face, though.

'All right, John?' he said.

'Yeah,' I said.

But I wasn't. I SO wasn't.

⭐ Me and God ⭐

Lord God, I know Jesus knows about suffering. I know He knows what it's like to be called names and pushed around because of You. I know He never let You down and He never stopped sticking up for You and doing what You wanted Him to do, even though it meant He was going to die. I do know all that stuff Dad said.

It's just that Dixons make me feel as if I'm a grungy old bit of rubbish and I don't know how to stand up to them. If it's all to do with me being part of Topz and going to church then maybe it'd be better if I didn't go so much so they'd stop picking on me. It's not that I want to stop being Your friend, it's just that I can't deal with them treating me like some sort of scaredy wet fish all the time. It wasn't like this for Jesus. He's powerful. He's brilliant.

And I'm just not.

I'm not anything.

17 JULY — MONDAY

Everyone's been going on about Paul's dad being a secret superhero.

Benny said, 'You know what? You really should check under his bed for a cape with a big S on it.'

Josie said, 'He probably hasn't

got one otherwise he would have been wearing it at the park.'

Paul said, 'Actually it explains an awful lot. I always wondered where I got my hero-type qualities. I'm obviously a superhero under development.'

'Or not,' said Mr Mallory, who unfortunately overheard him as he breezed past.

My den
Even Paul and his dad are powerful. What happened to me?

My den – later
Sarah said to me, 'Why are you so quiet all the time again?'

Mum said, 'Sarah's right, you know, you are quiet again.'

Sarah said, 'And if anyone should notice how quiet you're being, it's me because I'm the one you're always going on at.'

Mum said, 'Believe me, when John goes on at you, Sarah, he may as well be going on at me because I still get it full blast in both ears.'

Sarah said, 'It's not the same, though, because if you're not the one being gone on at you can close your ears and not listen.'

Mum said, 'The day I can close my ears and not listen to what goes on in this house is the day I turn into a … daffodil.'

Sarah paused, then, 'Why a daffodil?' she asked.

'Because,' answered Mum, 'they're an absolute picture after a long winter and they smell gorgeous. Just like me.'

'Right,' said Sarah. 'So anyway, John, why are you so quiet all the time again?'

'I'm not,' I said. 'Again.'

In bed

I wish they hadn't noticed but I suppose it's hard not to notice when someone isn't talking much. Only the reason I'm not talking is because I'm thinking. And the reason I'm thinking is because I've got to make a plan. I hate the way Dixons look at me as if I'm a scaredy wet fish, and I've got to work out a way to get them to stop it. Not that I've got anything against fish, scaredy or not. I think they're really cool the way they can sort of hover in one place underwater and open and close their mouths at you. It's just that's not how I want Dixons to look at me.

Ricky said I was scared. Too scared to go down the park on my own. Well, I'm not. I'm honestly not. And tomorrow after school – I'm going to prove it.

18 JULY — TUESDAY

Why is it the more you want everyone to keep their beaky noses out, the more they try and stick them in? Even Mr Mallory said, 'John, if you get any quieter, I shall be forced to think you've accidentally slipped into a ghastly black hole never to be heard from again.' (What does that man have for breakfast?)

Anyway, a black hole doesn't actually sound so bad. At least in black holes you can probably be quiet without anyone commenting on how quiet you are every five minutes.

Help!

Help!

Help!

4.30pm

Just pumped up my bike tyres. Heading off for the park soon. On my owny-o. I thought I'd try some stunts in the skateboard park. The Dixons might be there, they might not. Don't care much either way. I'm certainly not scared.

Sarah asked, 'Do you want to go two-player on the Playstation?'

'No, thanks,' I said. 'I'm going down the park.'

'Are you taking Gruff?' she said.

'No, I'm going on my bike,' I said.

'Can I come?' she said.

'No,' I answered. 'I want to go on my own.'

'That's not very nice,' she said.

'Why not?' I said. 'What's wrong with wanting to go on my own?'

'Because I've got nothing to do,' Sarah moaned.

'So?' I snapped. 'Look, Sarah, I can't always be hanging around with you. Just because we're twins doesn't mean we have to do every single boggly-eyed thing together.'

'We don't <u>actually</u> do every single boggly-eyed thing together most of the time,' Sarah snapped back.

'Good!' I said. 'Because sometimes I want to be JUST JOHN!'

4.45pm

Going now.
To the park.
On my own.
Without anyone else.
Not even Gruff.
If the Dixons don't show up, fine.

If they do … fine.

It's not like I'm scared or anything.

In bed

All Sarah said to me when I got home was, 'I hope you had a horrible time in the park without me, <u>Just John</u>.'

'No, I didn't, if you want to know,' I said. 'It was great. Ace. Fantasmagorical. I'm good on my own.'

'That's handy,' she said, 'because from now on that's what you're going to be – ON YOUR OWN.'

Later

Dad just came into my den.

He said, 'Time you lay down to sleep, I think.'

I said, 'Yeah, I will soon.'

He said, 'Is everything all right? You still seem very quiet.' (Aaagh! I mean, seriously, is there anyone on the planet who isn't interested in my noise levels?) 'No more problems with someone being called names for being a Christian?'

'No,' I grunted. 'Anyway, it wasn't a problem, I was just asking.'

'OK,' Dad said.

'Yup,' I said.

'Right.'

'Yeah.'

'Night night, John.'

'Night night, Dad.'

19 JULY — WEDNESDAY

6.00am

I knew they'd be there. The Dixons. They seem to be everywhere I go lately. I'd only been in the skateboard park five minutes yesterday and there they were, pointing at me and smirking.

'What's his problem?' I heard Clyde snigger. 'Doesn't he know the difference between a bike and a skateboard?'

'Maybe he does,' grinned Ricky. 'Maybe riding his bike in the skateboard park is John's idea of being naughty.'

'Yeah!' scoffed Kevin. 'Big, bad John, eh? I don't think so. Hey, Johnny! Give us a go on your bike.'

Uh oh, I thought. I guess this is it. This is my chance to stand up to them. Either that or it's the end of my bike. Whatever happens, I'm on my own. There's no one else here. Just me and the Dixons. Oh, help …

I pulled up by the railings next to them.

'I can't,' I said. 'Things … get broken when you're around. So I can't.'

Clyde stared at me. 'D'you really think we want to break your bike?' he said. 'We only want a go.'

'Well … I can't give you a go,' I answered. 'Anyway, I was just leaving.'

I wonder if they've noticed, I kept thinking. I wonder if they've noticed that I'm here on my own. They must know I'm not scared of them now.

'No, don't go yet, Johnny,' said Kevin.

For just a second, I thought he was starting to be more friendly. But then he opened his mouth again and that's when I realised – Kevin probably doesn't even know how to spell friendly.

'Tell you what,' he went on, 'this could be your chance to do something REALLY naughty.'

What now?

'Why don't you take your little bike,' he went on, 'and ride it down the slides in the toddler park?'

I swallowed and shook my head.

'No,' I said. 'You're not allowed to. You can get fined and everything.'

'Can you?' said Kevin, pretending to look shocked. 'Oh, no!'

'Don't worry,' said Ricky. 'We'll keep an eye out for you. Go on. I dare you.'

They were all staring at me. It was making my skin itch. Maybe coming here on my own wasn't such a good idea after all. What if they didn't let me go? I guessed the only thing I could do was try and make a break for it.

'I can't,' I said, 'I've got to get home.'

I pushed my left foot down hard on the pedal and powered off as fast as I could. I reckoned they were all pretty fast runners, but then I'm pretty fast on my bike so I thought they'd really have to go some to catch me.

As it turned out, they didn't catch me because they didn't bother trying. But then, they didn't have to. They did all the damage they needed when Clyde shouted after me, 'That's it, run away! You're such a sad, boring, little goody-goody, John! Loser!'

I could still hear them laughing at me when I got back to the zebra crossing.

I can still hear them laughing at me now ...

My den
Just had breakfast.

Sarah came into the kitchen and said, 'What are you doing in here?'

I said, 'Having breakfast. What does it look like?'

She said, 'Yes, but why are you having it in here? I thought you wanted to do everything on your own.'

Girls and slugs. Bleaahh.

4.30pm – Back in my den
At break, Dave said, 'Are you up for a Topz leapfrog relay after lunch?'

'Not really,' I said.

'Oh, come on,' he said. 'If us two team up, we'll be unbeatable like last time.'

'I don't want to,' I said. 'Why not?' he said.

'I just don't feel very ... froggy ... that's all.'

Well, what's wrong with that? To tell the truth, I don't feel very Topzy either. Like I said to Sarah, just because I'm twins with her, it doesn't mean we have to do everything together. It's the same with the Gang. Just because I'm in Topz doesn't mean that everything I do has to be Topzy.

4.40pm

What is it with everybody? If I'm not being a twin, I seem to have to be a Topz, and if I'm not being a Topz, I seem to have to be a twin. That's the whole problem with the Dixons, I'm sure of it. They don't look at me for who I am, they look at me for who everyone else is. And I'm not everyone else, I'm me. When, oh when, oh WHEN will anyone start to see me as JUST JOHN?

21 JULY — FRIDAY

Got home from school to find something quite alarming – there's an exercise bike in front of the TV.

I found Mum in the kitchen. Something else alarming – she was wearing trackie bottoms and trainers. Mum never wears trackie bottoms and trainers … unless … oh, no.

I said, 'Mum, there seems to be an exercise bike in the lounge.'

'Well spotted,' she said.

'And it's there because …?'

'Because, my little bundle of energy,' she announced, 'Mummy is getting fit!'

I knew it. The trackie bottoms and trainers said it all. Great. That means good-bye ice cream. So long double chocolate chip cookies. Farewell crisps. And as for pizza … dream on. From now on it'll be all bean sprouts and cous cous. Still, I suppose it won't be for long. Mum's fitness splurges never last.

I said hopefully, 'Yeah, but don't you remember the last time and that "stretch your way to fitness" class? You only went about once and then you said, "Stretch your way to fitness? Stretch your way to a serious injury more like." And that was the end of that.'

'Yes, thanks for bringing that up, John,' she said. 'Anyway, this is different. This is cycling. Not only that, but I get to watch all my favourite television programmes at the same time.'

'Yeah, but if you want to cycle, why not get a proper bike and go outside?'

'Because outside, people would be able to see me,' Mum said, 'and I don't want anyone seeing me until I'm fit enough to do it properly.'

'Right,' I said. 'I don't suppose there are any biscuits?'

'No,' she answered, 'but if you want a snack there's a tub of bean sprouts in the top of the fridge.'

Yay.

My den

Oh, well, at least Sarah's happy. When she saw Mum's bike she squealed. Very loudly. She also said now I could have my own way and go cycling down the park on my own whenever I wanted, because she'd be too busy cycling whenever she wanted without even having to leave the house.

There's another reason she's happy. She and Josie only went and won that design-a-cover competition for the new school information pack. She won't stop going on about it.

I said, 'Yes, but it was flowers. You drew flowers and Mrs Parker said it was really clever. How on earth can flowers say anything positive about Holly Hill School? Unless you're trying to put people off. What's so clever about that?'

'They're not any old flowers,' Sarah said, 'they're daisies. And the clever part is that some of them are just buds, and what that says about our school is that you start there as a little kid when you're four or something (a bud, in other words), and by the time you leave you've blossomed into a daisy – a grown up kid. Not completely grown up, obviously, because that would be like Mum or Dad and they'd just look silly at primary school, but more than when you started.'

'Are you telling me I'm going to grow up to be a daisy?' I said.

'No, of course not,' snapped Sarah. 'You're <u>deliberately</u> not understanding. You're just jealous because you didn't even bother to enter the competition.'

'I was going to enter the competition,' I said, 'I've just … had a lot to think about.'

'Oh, yeah, like what?' Sarah demanded.

'Never mind,' I grunted. 'Anyway, you know what most people call daisies, don't you?'

'No, what?'

'Weeds.'

Still in my den
Dave rang.

He said, 'You are still coming to youth club tonight, aren't you?'

I said, 'Yes, why wouldn't I be?'

He said, 'Well, I'm not being funny or anything, but you seem to be trying to avoid us.'

'I'm not trying to avoid anybody,' I said. 'Sometimes I just want a bit of space, that's all.'

'OK,' he said. 'See you there.'

Youth club's OK. Lots of kids go to youth club. It's not just Topz. It's not just church. It's anyone. It's somewhere I can be just me. Not only that, but there's going to be a trip on tomorrow. Greg just hasn't told us where we're going yet. Youth club's cool. <u>And</u> there'll be chips not bean sprouts.

In bed
Unbelievable. The other kids at youth club are UNBELIEVABLE.

!!!

I seriously cannot believe what happened.

It's <u>so</u> unbelievable, it's not even worth writing down.

I mean, there's no point wasting paper with it.

***

OK, what happened was, just before we all got stuck in, Greg said, 'Right, you lot. You've got a choice for the trip tomorrow – bowling or ice-skating. Have a think and we'll take a vote on it at the end of the evening.'

Zippety zonkas, I thought. Glad I came to youth

club. I just fancy going bowling. We haven't done that for ages. I'll whip round and have a word with a few Topzies – make sure the vote goes the bowling way.

I said to Dave, 'Think bowling's a wicked idea. How about you?'

'Yeah,' he said. 'Like the idea of the ice-skating, too.'

I said to Benny, 'Yo, Benny! You don't want to do ice-skating, do you?'

'Haven't decided, yet,' he said. 'You'll have to wait till the vote.'

I said to Danny, 'How about you, Danny? Come on, ice-skating's for girls.'

'I'm still thinking,' he said.

Then Paul said he wasn't sure, although the last time he went bowling, he'd dropped a ball on his foot, so from the point of view of not doing that again, he'd be happy to be a girl, and I knew it wasn't even worth asking Sarah and Josie, who are, after all, girls. I tried scouting round some of the other youth clubbers, but none of them seemed to be able to make up their minds either.

So, when it was time to vote, guess what happened?

Greg said, 'OK, who's for bowling?'

Only two of us stuck our hands up – me and Matt Cartwright. And even then Matt put his down again the second he saw that everyone else was obviously going to vote for the girly thing – which on Greg's, 'And who's for ice-skating?', they all immediately did. I mean, what is this, a youth club or a sheep farm?

We're going ice-skating!

So thanks, Topz, thanks a lot. You knew what I wanted and you still went the other way. It's great to know who your friends really are.

Dave said, 'Sorry, John, but ice-skating'll be fun. You should still come.'

I said, 'Forget it. Anyway, it just goes to prove my theory.'

He said, 'What theory's that?'

I said, 'It doesn't matter.'

Well, it doesn't. Not to Dave, not to anyone else. I'm the one it matters to. Just me. Just John. And it's so simple I don't know why I haven't realised it before –

I'm not so sure I'm cut out for the Topz Gang any more.

22 JULY — SATURDAY
NON-TOPZ DAY 1

⭐ Me and God ⭐

Lord God, just because I've decided to leave the Topz Gang doesn't mean I'm not going to be Your friend any more. Being in Topz or not being in Topz doesn't make a difference to me and You one way or another.

Anyway, I've been thinking. The Topzies were all quite happy to leave me on my own and do the swimming gala. Now they're all quite happy to go off ice-skating without me when they know I want go bowling. Maybe they don't actually want me in the Gang any more, they just don't know how to tell me. After all, they've still got Sarah. And Sarah's the clever one who wins Holly Hill School information pack cover competitions. I'm just the nerd. So that works out great. I want to leave. They don't want me to stay. Splendividosi. Everyone's a winner.

It's just … I thought winning was supposed to feel good.

10.30am

Dave rang.

He said, 'Please come ice-skating this afternoon. We can fix up to go bowling another time.'

'No, it's OK,' I said. 'I've got stuff to do anyway.'

'What stuff?' he asked.

'Just stuff,' I said.

'What, on your own?' he said.

'Maybe, maybe not,' I said. 'Why d'you care so much?'

'Of course I care,' he said. 'You're my mate. Anyway, you're one of the Gang.'

'Yes, about that,' I said. 'Maybe not so much one of the Gang any more.'

'What's that supposed to mean?'

'What does it sound like?'

'Sounds like you're saying you want to leave Topz.'

'That must be it, then.'

'But why?' Dave said. I suppose he sounded upset, I don't know. He was probably just pretending.

'Because,' I answered.

'Because what?' Dave went on. 'You can't want to leave just because we don't want to go bowling.'

'Of course not,' I said. 'I'm not that much of a baby. How could you even think that? It's just … I want to be just John. I want other people to look at me as just

John. Not John the Topzy, John the twin, John the anything else. And none of you lot want me any more anyway, so that's all fine.'

'What are you talking about?' Dave demanded. 'Whatever gives you the idea we don't want you any more?'

'Look, I've really got to go,' I said. 'Have a great time ice-skating.'

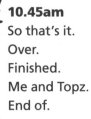

10.45am
So that's it.
Over.
Finished.
Me and Topz.
End of.

My den

There I was, on my own, minding my own business, like I do in my den, when suddenly Sarah slammed open the door and marched in angrily like Mr Mallory hunting for a lost library book.

She yelled, 'You have just ruined my afternoon ice-skating!'

I said, 'How can I possibly have done that? I've been in my den.'

'Exactly!' she shouted. 'That's where you are all the time these days. And it's not a den, it's a bedroom. And if it <u>was</u> a den, you'd be a bear, or something! And what d'you mean by telling Dave you're leaving Topz?'

Later

I wish I <u>was</u> a bear. How cool would that be? That would get everyone to leave me alone because if they didn't, I could scare them all away by running around after them showing my teeth and roaring or whatever that sound is they make.

Mmm. Could be worth a try even though I'm <u>not</u> a bear …

In bed

I love my dad. When I grow up I want to be just like him. He may not always understand what's going on in my head, but he always wants to help. Obviously he can't really help this time because I've got to do it on my own. I like the things he says, though.

He sat on my bed and said, 'I know it seems as if Sarah's angry with you, but she's not really. She's upset. Very upset. She's worried about you. We all are.'

'There's no need to be,' I shrugged. 'I'm fine. Honest.'

'That's good,' Dad said. 'After all, it's almost the summer holidays. If you can't be fine when you're about to have six weeks off school, then when can you be?'

'Exactly,' I said.

'I'm a bit surprised you've chosen now to leave Topz, though,' he went on. 'I mean, all those days off. Normally you'd be out there with the Gang doing all that stuff you like to do together. You're going to miss all that. And, if that's not going to happen this holiday, how are you planning to fill your time?'

'Don't know, yet,' I answered. Well, I don't. I've only just decided to become a non-Topz. I can't sort everything out at once. 'It's OK, though,' I said. 'I'm good on my own.'

'I'm sure you are,' Dad said, 'but, what I don't quite understand is that you don't have to be on your own. You've got me and your mum and Sarah, and you've got your friends. Why are you trying to push us all away? Why do you want to isolate yourself? It can't be much fun on Planet Lonely.'

'But that's the whole point,' I said, 'I'm not lonely. I like it. It's … fun. And it'll prove to everyone that I'm worth something on my own. Just me. Just John.'

Dad frowned. 'And why would you want to prove something like that?' he asked. 'More to the point, who are you trying to prove it to?'

'No one,' I said. 'It doesn't matter.'

He was quiet for a moment, then went on, 'Being part of Topz isn't just about having friends to mess around with. The reason why Topz is so special and so good for you is because you're all Christians. You've all got God as your best friend. You all talk to Him. You all love Him. And, most of the time, you try and keep Him at the centre of everything you do. Having friends who believe the same as you do is important. Spending time with them matters. It means you can all support and encourage one another, and pray for each other, too. That's why people who love God go to church – to be with one another. To learn about God and to talk to Him – together. As a family. Because that's what we are: we're God's family. We need each other.'

You see, that's where I think I'm different to other

people. I honestly don't think I need anyone. I've got Gruff and I've got my bike. There must be loads of things I could go and do on my own, I just don't think of doing them because I'm always doing stuff with Topz.

And I can still talk to God without being in a gang. I talk to Him on my own a lot anyway.

Like I said to Dad, it's OK, I'm good on my own.

He still doesn't quite get it, though.

He said, 'Yes, well, sounds an awful lot like Planet Lonely to me.'

23 JULY — SUNDAY
NON-TOPZ DAY 2

☆ Me and God ☆

This is it, then, Lord God: day 2. It's not bad actually. Dad's wrong. I am <u>so</u> not lonely. I just wish I didn't have to go to church today. Nothing to do with You or anything, it's just they'll all start on at me. All the Topz Gang. All of them together. <u>Why have you left Topz? What's wrong? How come you don't want to hang around with us anymore?</u> And on and on. Blah, blah, blah.

Still, at least at Sunday Club I can just be my own individual person now – sit next to who I want; talk to who I want; be partners with who I want; or not. It's up to me. My life is my own. I am officially a non-Topz. Yippety yonkas.

And when the Dixons find out, they might even think I'm cool.

My den

They don't believe me. Topzies. Some of them anyway.
They think I'm messing around.

Paul, for example, said, 'Good one, John. You almost
had me going for a minute.'

Benny, for another, said, 'How do you do it?'

I said, 'How do I do what?'

He said, 'Keep a straight face.'

I said, 'Simple. I'm not joking.'

He said, 'Yeah, right.'

Danny hasn't said a word, he's just been looking at
Dave. Dave's been trying not to look at anyone, and
Josie and Sarah have been really obviously moping
about. One of them must have said something to Greg,
though, because he knew all about me being a non-
Topz.

I wasn't planning on talking to Greg today
particularly. I really couldn't be bothered with
another whole 'What's all this about you and Topz?'
conversation. Only he said some seriously interesting
stuff at Sunday Club and it got me thinking, like
seriously interesting stuff does.

Greg was telling us how God gives us the Holy Spirit
to help make us brave – to help give us the confidence
to talk to others about Him. He showed us in the Bible
(in the book of 2 Timothy, chapter 1, verse 7) where it
says, 'For the Spirit that God has given us does not make
us timid; instead, his Spirit fills us with power, love, and
self-control.' He said that Jesus' disciples weren't strong,
brave people. They were ordinary like us.

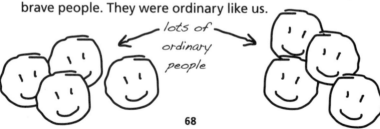

lots of
ordinary
people

They had worries and fears like we do. They could be selfish. They wasted time arguing about silly little things. But when Jesus had gone back up to heaven, God sent the Holy Spirit to fill them, and suddenly they were brave and powerful and no one could stop them talking about Jesus!

So I said to Greg afterwards, 'Can I chat to you sometime?'

He said, 'You can chat to me now if you want.'

I said, 'OK. What it is is … I don't feel powerful. I don't feel much good at anything when I think about it. I'm not as clever as Sarah (not that I'd ever tell her that). I don't even think I fit in with other people the way she does. In fact, I just don't think I'm the sort of person God can use for anything. I mean, the disciples may have been ordinary, but I'm even more ordinary than that.'

'Good,' Greg said (rather surprisingly, I thought), 'because that makes you <u>exactly</u> the sort of person God wants to use to do powerful things.'

Huh?

'Jesus isn't looking for wealthy, important, famous, <u>powerful</u> people to work with Him. Look at the disciples. Those were twelve ordinary men He chose. Fishermen. One of them was a tax collector. There was nothing especially exciting about their lives – or about them. They were simply ordinary people, people who probably, like you, didn't think they'd ever do anything special because that's not the sort of lives they led.

'Only God thought differently. He knew exactly how

many special things they were going to be able to do for Him. And when He sent His Holy Spirit to live in those disciples, He filled them with all the power they'd need to go out and let the world know about Him. We may think we're pretty pathetic at times and no good at all – but God can use us because that's what He does. He uses people no one would expect. Think about when Jesus was born. Who were the first ones to hear about Him? God didn't send His angels to tell the rich, important people that His Son had been born on earth. He sent them to tell some shepherds; some poor, lowly shepherds who would have had barely a penny between them and probably hadn't had a bath in a month of Sundays.

'What you need to do, John, is to try not to think about all your bad points, all your weaknesses. God's not thinking about those. He's looking at all the wonderful things you'll be able to do for Him using His strength. Ask Him to fill you with His Holy Spirit and believe that He will. Then you might be amazed at the things you can do for Him.'

'That would be cool,' I said, 'to be amazed at yourself.'

'It can happen,' said Greg. 'I'm amazed I'm a church youth leader. Never thought I had it in me – until God uncovered it. And what's brilliant about God is that whatever work He sends us to do, whatever He wants to make us powerful for, He will be with us. He says so in the Bible. Several times. "I will be with you."'

Wow. That is all so great. In fact, it would have been the perfect conversation if Greg hadn't followed it up with, 'I'm not sure what's going on with you and Topz, but I hope you don't stay away for too long. Being part of a group doesn't make you any less of a person. You can be in the Gang and still be just John. Not that <u>you</u> could ever be "just" anything,' he added. 'You're too much of a nutty noodle for that.'

Yeah, well, I thought but didn't say out loud, what happens with me and Topz is up to me. There's no point talking about it. No one'll ever understand.

Then suddenly Greg said, 'Can I just say a quick prayer?'

I wasn't expecting that. Greg's prayed with me before, but today I didn't know whether I wanted him to or not. So I shuffled about a bit.

'Won't take a minute,' he said.

'OK,' I mumbled thinking, just please don't ask God to put me back in Topz.

He didn't.

He prayed, 'Dear Lord God, thank You that You love ordinary people like John and like me. Thank You that we don't have to be anything particularly important to get You to notice us and love us, because You love us just as we are. Thank You that You can take our ordinariness and turn it into extraordinariness with Your Holy Spirit. Help John to understand that and to know that he is so special to You. Amen.'

'Amen,' I said quietly.

When we'd finished and I went to find Mum and Dad, there was Sarah hanging around just outside the door.

'What was all that about?' she demanded.

'Nothing,' I shrugged.
'Fine, then, don't tell me.'
'Fine, then, I won't.'

25 JULY — TUESDAY
NON-TOPZ DAY 4

Last day of term! More to the point,
LAST DAY OF MR MALLORY FOR SIX
WHOLE WEEKS!! Although I have
to say that, as teachers go, he does
do pretty amazing last days of term.
That's why I'm sitting waiting for the
bus in one of Dad's stripey T-shirts,
with two sticky-up ears on my head
and a long tail hanging off my belt.
Sarah says she's not sitting next to me.

Apparently, Mrs Parker's letting her class do painting
and write poems as an end of term 'treat' or something,
which is quite sad but fine for someone like Sarah
because she's really into all that stuff. But Mr Mallory's
had a much more totally stonking idea. He says we
don't have to wear school uniform today but can come
dressed up as a character from our favourite book.

'Wicked!' I said.

'Yeah!' said Benny.

'Who are you going to be?' said Ryan.

Which is when I realised. I don't actually have a
favourite book.

'Well,' I said, 'who are <u>you</u> going to be?'

'I reckon it'd be pretty cool to be Long John Silver out
of "Treasure Island",' Ryan answered.

'Triple yeah!' shrieked Benny. 'That means I could be
your parrot!'

'You could, I suppose,' nodded Ryan, 'but there's no
way you're sitting on my shoulder, all right?'

Benny said why didn't I dress up as a pirate and

bouncy

bouncy

bouncy

bouncy

then we could all be characters out of 'Treasure Island' together, but I said no, it was fine and I'd come up with something on my own.

He said, 'Why do you want to do <u>everything</u> on your own these days?'

I said, 'Because I can. I'm good on my own.'

Trouble was, I didn't seem to be that good at coming up with a book character on my own, so in the end I asked Mum.

She said, 'How about Winnie-the-Pooh out of "Winnie-the-Pooh"?'

Which gave me a BRILLIANT idea. How about Tigger out of 'Winnie-the-Pooh'? I mean, zippety stonkers! That's got to be better than being a parrot.

I said, 'Mum, you are a

⋝JENIUS⋜

– with a capital J!'

She said, 'I think you'll find that's

⋝GENIUS⋜

with a capital G. But thanks anyway.'

You see, it's not that 'Winnie-the-Pooh' is my favourite book (although I do really like it because Mum used to read it to us a lot when we were little – with all the different voices and everything, and Sarah said that when she grew up, she wanted to be Piglet), it's just that it means I can spend the whole day bouncing. Bouncing isn't something I get to do much of in Mr Mallory's class. I don't think Mr Mallory ever bounces anywhere himself. He's a bit too ploddy.

So anyway, last night Mum helped me sort out what I was going to wear. She dug out Dad's old stripey T-shirt and hacked the bottom off because otherwise it would have hung down past my knees and not looked very Tigger-like. Unfortunately that's not the only thing that makes it not very Tigger-like. The stripes are blue and white instead of orange and black, but Mum says, if anyone asks, I can just say I'm being Tigger on a cold day. Then she cut one leg off a pair of tights, twisted it round, tied a knot in both ends and got me to colour black stripes all down it with a fabric pen to make my tail. Last of all, for my ears, she sewed two pointy bits of black felt onto one of Sarah's hair bands.

I tied the tail onto a belt which is going round my middle and said to Sarah when I was all dressed up, 'OK, who am I?'

She said, 'A rather tragic person with an even more tragic dress sense?'

I am so right. Girls and slugs. One and the same. Not only are they both icky and slimy, but they've just got no imagination.

5.00pm
Great last day of term. Great, great, GREAT last day!

I went into class and everyone, but everyone, was in fancy dress. It was like walking into a circus. Even Mr Mallory was dressed up – as, if you can believe it, the white rabbit from 'Alice in Wonderland'! I never in a million years thought he'd get into a costume as well. I mean, come on, this is Mr Mallory we're talking about, all times tables and spellings and incredibly boring facts about all sorts of incredibly boring stuff that's designed to bore you incredibly. But he was brilliant. He kept rushing around, wrinkling up his nose and going, 'Dear, dear, dear, look at the time, I'm late!' He was honestly just like in the film I've seen. Danny said he was so realistic, he wished he'd brought in a carrot from his dad's allotment. Benny, who was actually quite impressive as a parrot, said could Danny maybe start bringing in carrots next term anyway because, after all, they're delicious and you don't have to be a rabbit to enjoy them.

In between all the rushing and nose-wrinkling, Mr Mallory was going round giving everyone a piece of paper with all our names on and space for writing up to three guesses as to who each person was dressed up as, and which book the character came from. I knew who Benny and Ryan were meant to be, and some of the others were pretty obvious, but with quite a few people it was total guesswork.

The problem was, my identity turned out to be such total guesswork that that's how it stayed – total guesswork. And all completely wrong. Everyone got guessed by someone – except me. All the guesses about me were things like:

CHARACTER	BOOK
A burglar	From a book about burgling (or something).
An alien	From an alien sort of book.
A weird monster	Weird monster book.
A creepy plant (!!)	Book about gardening in space.
Cricket-playing person (!!!)	Cricket fashion book.

I mean, come on guys! Whoever saw a cricketer with a tail? Or a creepy plant with ears? Or a weird monster in a stripy T-shirt? Or an alien or a burglar who look like TIGGER ON A COLD DAY?

'Oh,' said Benny. 'Is that who you're meant to be? Tigger on a cold day?'

Urrgh.

At break, Sarah said, 'So? Did everyone know who you're supposed to be?'

I said, 'Not exactly.'

Benny said, 'Not at all.'

Sarah said, 'I knew it. And I'm not sitting next to you on the bus on the way home either.'

For the rest of the day, we did quizzes, watched a DVD and played this odd game involving some astonishingly bad hats which Mr Mallory said he'd found at a car boot sale. (No one believed they weren't his, though. In fact all the girls reckoned he'd probably got a cupboard full of astonishingly bad shoes to go with them, and always got them out to wear together on special occasions like his birthday and at Christmas.)

Benny, Danny and Ryan wanted me on their team for the hat game, but I decided to go with Marcus, Liam and Chelsea. It was nice of the others to want me and everything, but it would be silly to be Topzy in school and non-Topzy out of school. I've just got to show everyone I am who I am now. Branching out, Dad would call it. They'll get the hang of it in the end.

Benny said, 'You have to keep making a point, don't you? Are you really leaving Topz?'

I said, 'I'm not making a point about anything, and I've already left.'

26 JULY — WEDNESDAY
NON-TOPZ DAY 5

Typical. First day of the summer holidays and what's it doing? Pouring with rain. Throwing it down. By the bucketful. It's been doing it all night. Thunder and lightning and everything. I heard Sarah go into Mum and Dad. She always does that when we get thunderstorms at night. She hates them. She says they make the sky sound angry and why can't they just rumble away and leave us alone.

I said, 'Now you know how I feel living with you.'

She flicked some Rice Krispies at me and rumbled, 'Yes, well, you're just a big, grumpy … fishcake!'

Saucy doesn't seem to like thunderstorms either. She hasn't eaten her breakfast.

My den

Been making a plan called 'Things To Do On My Own'. It's going quite well. I'm beginning to wonder where I'm going to find the time to cram everything in. So far I've got:

* Walk Gruff twice a day.
* Go to the shop when Mum wants milk or other stuff (although sadly not buns or biscuits because she's still doing the bean sprout thing).
* Zip to the park on my bike.
* Maybe try out the exercise bike (when no one's around).
* Write my wacky diary.
* Wash my bike if it's got muddy in the park.
* Mend my skateboard (although I might have to get Dad to help me).
* Read (not sure what, but something).
* Play on Playstation.
* Goalie practice in the park.
* Watch TV.

77

Good, eh? The list is endless – until it comes to an end, obviously. The next step is to work out a timetable showing when I'm going to do what, which worries me slightly because it's a bit like the sort of thing Mr Mallory would do but, hey, if it works for him, it can work for me. It doesn't mean I have to start being boring and collecting astonishingly bad hats.

10.15am
OK. Done the timetable. Might have to have a re-think, though. I'm down for cycling in the park now and it's still raining. Hmph.

11.00am
✓ Done a bit of reading.
✓ Watched TV.
✓ Played on the Playstation.
Dum de dum de dum.
I am SO NOT bored, though.

11.15am

Sarah's gone round to Josie's.

I said to Mum, 'Can't she last five minutes without having to be with someone else?'

Mum said, 'Not everyone wants to hide themselves away in a bucket, you know.'

'I am not hiding away,' I said. 'I am being myself.'

11.20am – Back in my den

Parents. They just don't understand. They think that because they used to be children once (apparently) they know everything about us. Well, they don't. I'm not hiding. I'm having a great time. I can do what I want when I want. No one bothering me to go anywhere. No one ringing me up. No one the slightest bit interested. Yaayy.

11.25am

I wonder what Sarah and Josie are doing. Not that I care or anything. It's probably something incredibly boring and nothing like I'd want to be doing at all.

11.30am

I said to Mum, 'D'you want to play Snap?'

'Can't, sorry,' she said. 'I've got a pile of ironing to do.'

'Shall I go to the shop, then?' I asked.

'We don't need anything,' she answered.

'Well, shall I hang out the washing?'

'What, in this weather?'

'I could always hoover.'

'Thanks, but Sarah's done it.'

'Do you want me to make some lunch?'

'It's a bit early, yet.'

'Well, there must be something I can do,' I moaned.

'John,' she sighed, 'it's wonderful that you want to be so helpful and it's not that I don't appreciate it because I do, I really do. But at the moment, there's nothing waiting to be done. And if you're so bored, why on earth don't you go and do something with the Gang?'

'Because I'm not in the Gang any more,' I snapped. 'And anyway, I'm NOT BORED!'

My den

Sarah's still not back. Can't imagine what she and Josie have to do all the time. Silly, girly, sluggy stuff, I suppose.

After lunch

Dave rang.

He said, 'Hi.'

I said, 'Hi.'

He said, 'Are you busy?'

I said, 'Yeah. Tons of stuff.'

He said, 'Wicked.'

I said, 'You bet.'

He said, 'Anyway, the thing is ... I mean, I didn't ask you before because of you leaving Topz and everything ... and I know you've got loads of stuff planned on your own, so you probably wouldn't be able to fit it in ... and you might think it's a bit too Topzy even though the only two Topz doing it are me and Paul ... and I don't want you to think I'm being pushy, because I'm not trying to be ... after all, if you don't want to have anything to do with us any more, then that's up to you –'

'Er – Dave,' I interrupted.

'Yes?' he said.

'What?'

'It's just Boys' Brigade have got a barbeque and sleepover in the hall planned for tomorrow and I wondered if you wanted to come.'

'Cool,' I said.

'We were going to camp but Greg says it'll probably be too wet.'

'He's probably right,' I said.

'So ... do you think you might?'

'Not sure,' I said. 'I'll have to see what I'm doing. I've got a list. You know how it is. But thanks anyway.'

'No worries,' he said.

My den

Maybe I'll go, maybe I won't.

I mean, I've got so much planned already, I'll have to see if I can fit it into my positively packed, all on my owney-o timetable.

Still, I suppose I could do the <u>odd</u> thing with the <u>odd</u> Topz at the <u>odd</u> time. It's not as if one little overnight campy thing makes me into a Topzy again, is it?

So why not?

The bathroom

Yes, I'm in the bathroom. Lying in the bath. Not with water in it or anything because I've still got my clothes on so that would be silly. I just wanted to know what it's like lying in the bath. Mum's the only one who has baths in our house. Which doesn't mean that the rest of us are filthy dirty and you can smell us coming from the next street, it's just we only ever have showers.

I thought I'd spend a bit of time in here to have a change of scene. Dens are groovy but sometimes you need to give them a rest. And if there's one thing our bathroom is, it's restful. Mum says it's all down to the green walls. She chose green to make her bath times more relaxing and this particular green is called 'Sage Moment'. I'm not sure whether this has something to do with having a bath and becoming more wise, or whether it's meant to be more herb-like but, whatever, I quite like lying in here and may consider having a bath once a week in the future. I could even add it to my timetable.

Still in the bathroom

Of course, nothing in the world can make a green bathroom relaxing when there's a sudden shriek from downstairs and your mum starts screaming, 'Oh, no! Just what I need on my new rug. Saucy's been sick!'

The other thing that kind of wipes out any possibility of relaxation is the smell of Dettol.

5.00pm

Sarah finally got home from Josie's about half an hour ago. She's gone again now. With Mum. And Saucy. To the vet.

I thought it was odd when Saucy didn't eat her breakfast. She hasn't done any snacking today either, which is so un-Saucyish. Normally she's pestering for food on and off all day long – quite often even when she's already got some snacks in a bowl, because they might happen to be tuna flavoured when what she fancies just at that moment is salmon. Very picky, cats. Not like Gruff. He just gobbles down whatever it is whenever it's there. Bit like me.

So anyway, (1) there was Saucy obviously not feeling very well at all, (2) there was Sarah coming home and being told by Mum that they ought to take her to the vet, and (3) there was me saying, 'Hang on a minute and I'll come with you,' and suddenly Sarah went into this totally major flip flop.

'You're NOT coming!' she screamed at me.

'What do you mean?' I asked, completely mystified, although it has to be said that most of what Sarah says is a complete mystery to me most of the time.

'Because,' she yelled, 'all you want is not to be my twin, not to be in Topz and not to have anything to do with anyone in the entire universe, past, present or future. So, guess what? You're <u>not</u> coming to the vet with Saucy because me and Mum want to take her

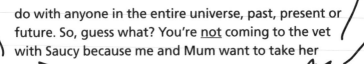

ON OUR OWN!!'

Mum raised her eyes at Dad like she does when Sarah goes off like a firework and said, almost calmly, 'We really don't have time to argue about this now. The vet will be closed in a minute.'

'Fine,' I shrugged. 'Go on your own. No probs. Just remember which one of us has been at home with Saucy all day while she's been feeling really grotty, and which one of us has been OUT.'

That was mean, actually. Really mean. Horrible. That was when Sarah started crying.

In bed

STILL raining. I've decided I'm not calling them the summer holidays any more. I'm calling them the 'wet season' holidays. School holidays in the winter I'm going to call the 'even wetter season' holidays. Although I think any day in winter would be hard pushed to throw down as much rain as we've had today.

Saucy's going to be all right. The vet says she's got some sort of stomach bug, probably because of eating something she shouldn't, and she's got to have this white, powdery stuff sprinkled on her food for a few days. She's had an injection and the vet reckons she should start getting her appetite back by tomorrow. If not, the powder's got to be mixed in water and squirted into her mouth. Not sure how that's going to work. Saucy's not the sort of cat to like having things squirted into her mouth, but Sarah says if she explains to her first that it's for her own good, there won't be a problem. Mmm ...

Sarah and me, we're OK again. For now, anyway. You can never tell how long we're going to be OK for, which is why Mum does a lot of sighing and eye raising and head shaking whenever we make up after a quarrel because she knows there's no point hoping the peace will last forever. But, like I say to her, I think that's all part of the exciting challenge of being a parent to more than one child and, actually, too much peace isn't good for anybody (probably).

So anyway, there I was talking to God after Sarah and Mum had gone to the vet, partly to ask Him to help Saucy to get better and partly to say I was sorry for being so nasty to Sarah, and I just know He was telling me I had to sort it out before bedtime. So I did.

I said to Sarah when they got back and she'd settled Saucy down on the sofa with a big blanket and some cushions, 'Do you want to come in my room for a minute?'

pong!

pong!

pong!

pong!

'Why would I want to do that?' she answered. 'It smells of old socks.'

'Fine,' I said. 'We'll talk in your room.'

'Why would I want you in <u>my</u> room?' she said. 'You smell of old socks, too.'

Which is when Mum called through from the kitchen, 'All right, you two, this is today's final warning.'

We ended up in the bathroom perched on the edge of the bath. It's not as comfortable as sitting on my bed and felt a bit as if we were a couple of pigeons on a window ledge, but I thought the 'Sage Moment' might have an important calming effect. As it turned out, I was right.

I said, 'Look, I know you probably don't care if I'm sorry or not, but I am sorry, I'm <u>really</u> sorry I was nasty to you about Saucy, because she still would have been ill whether you'd been here or not, and if you'd known she was ill I know you wouldn't have gone out, and anyway it's none of my business what you do or when you do it or where you go, and I should have just kept my mouth shut, and I will in future, and I really don't know what's wrong with me half the time at the moment, and I just wanted you to know, that's all.'

I stopped. Suddenly. I had to. I'd hardly taken a breath and I'd gone all dizzy. That's when I noticed Sarah was smiling. I smiled back. Then –

'You're so stupid!' she said.

'What?'

'Of course I care that you're sorry, but if I hadn't told you you couldn't come to the vet, you wouldn't have been nasty to me in the first place so you see, really it was all my fault and I'm the one who should be saying sorry to you.'

pong!

pong!

'Oh,' I said. 'I hadn't thought of it like that. So why don't you?'

'Why don't I what?'

'Say sorry.'

'I was going to, but then you went off jabbering like some crazy old jabbering noodle-head and I couldn't get a word in.'

'Right,' I said. 'Sorry.'

'Yes,' she answered. 'Well, I'm sorry too.'

'So am I.'

'I know.'

'Good.'

Then Sarah said, 'Would you do something for me?'

I said, 'What?'

She said, 'Would you pray with me? I want to ask God to help Saucy get better.'

'Oh, that's all right,' I said, 'I've already done that.'

'So have I, dimbo,' she said, 'but Jesus likes it when we pray about things together. He says where two or three come together and pray in His name, He'll be right there with them. And I want Him right there with us while we pray about Saucy.'

I felt funny. I hadn't thought about praying with anyone since I left Topz. Especially not Sarah. But she was sitting there looking at me, and if I'd said no she probably would have stomped off and, to be honest, I probably couldn't blame her.

'You pray, then,' I said, 'and I'll be doing it with you.'

⭐ Me and Sarah and God ⭐
(Sarah's prayer)

Dear Lord, thank You for Saucy and thank You for our vet. He's really kind, and if I was a sick cat there isn't a vet in the whole world I'd rather go to. Thank You that he's given Saucy stuff to help her get better. Please help her to be completely well very soon and back to her old greedy, fidgety, snugly self. It won't be the same without her waking me up in the middle of the night trying to take over my pillow. In fact I shall probably wake up in the night anyway just because she's not doing her snuggling thing and everything's too still.

And while we're here, I want to talk to You about John. I'm not sure why he doesn't want to do anything with Topz at the moment or why he thinks being all on his own somehow makes him a better person or whatever it is, but please help him to see that he's a brilliant person anyway. Help him to know how much Topz miss him and how much You love him. And please look after him, Lord, because he doesn't seem to want anyone else to. Thank You. Amen.

I didn't know what to say. I still don't know what to say. I wasn't expecting it. I couldn't believe Sarah cared that much. I think maybe I could be slightly wrong about the whole girls and slugs thing. It is possible girls have more feelings than slugs.

Sarah smiled at me. It was one of those moments when you almost feel you want to talk about things you really don't

Slugs have feelings too!

HUG A SLUG

want to talk about. So much so that I nearly started to tell her about the Dixons. But then I thought, nah, no point. I'm dealing with it.

'I'm going to check on Saucy now,' Sarah said.

'Great,' I said.

Everything's great. It's all just totally … well … great.

10.00pm

I wonder whether two or three have ever come together and prayed in a bathroom before.

27 JULY — THURSDAY
NON-TOPZ DAY 6

Dave rang.

He said, 'Not meaning to be annoying or anything because I know you're packed to the eyeballs with stuff to do and lists and all that, but I was just wondering if you'd decided whether you might like to do the Boys' Brigade sleepover tonight.'

'The thing is, I've been thinking about that,' I said, 'and what I've been thinking is we haven't had a good barbeque for ages and I don't think my sleeping bag's been out of the cupboard since last year.'

Dave said, 'Right.'

I said, 'And it's not even raining today.'

Dave said, 'I'd noticed.'

I said, 'And, to be honest, I could shuffle some of my list about because Dad always says lists should be flexible.'

Dave said, 'Whatever that means.'

I said, 'Exactly. And Sarah and I were getting on a

lot better yesterday now that Saucy's going to be all right and ate her breakfast with the white powder stuff sprinkled on and everything, although I think the "Sage Moment" in the bathroom might have had a lot to do with it.'

'Obviously,' said Dave, not sounding as though anything was obvious at all. 'So all that would mean …?'

'Yes,' I said. 'All that would mean yes.'

'Wicked,' said Dave. 'Pick you up at 5 o'clock.'

10.15am
Well, why not? Even non-Topzies can go on sleepovers with their mates. And that's what Dave is. A mate.

10.30am
I said to Sarah, 'Do you fancy coming for a walk with Gruff?'

She said, 'Really? You really want me to go with you?'

'Yeah,' I said. 'I think Gruff would like it. He had the mopes yesterday, partly because of the rain, but partly because he knew Saucy was ill, I reckon. I thought we could let him have a good run in the park. We could take the football and everything.'

'That would be so great,' she said, 'I mean really fantasticoco, it's just …'

'What?'

'It's just I think I should stay with Saucy. She's loads better but if I go out she might get lonely and stop eating again, whereas if I stay in and sit next to her munching Maltesers all day, she might get back to her usual snacky sort of self.'

'Just you and me, then,' I said to Gruff. Which is cool. After all, that's how I planned the wet season holidays. It's just that, after our bathroom moment yesterday I've been thinking that spending a teeny bit of time with Sarah probably won't interfere with me being just John.

My den

IT'S NOT FAIR. WHY DOES **EVERYTHING** ALWAYS HAVE TO GO BAD???

Den again

Rang Dave.

I said, 'Sorry. Changed my mind. Can't come tonight.'

Dave said, 'Why? What's happened?'

I said, 'Nothing's happened. Why does something have to have happened? Why can't it be that I just DON'T WANT TO COME?'

Bathroom

If ever I needed a 'Sage Moment' to help me relax, it's now. Only it's not working. I've been lying in the bath for five minutes and all I've got is a pain in my back and a stiff neck. I don't know why people enjoy lying in the bath. It really hurts on all those bony, knobbly bits like down your spine and on your elbows. It must be actually lying in water that makes it more comfortable, because otherwise nobody would bother and bath makers everywhere would have to close down.

Sarah's in a mood with me.

She knocked on the door and said, 'I don't know what you're doing but could you come out now, please, so that I can have a shower?'

I said, 'I'll come out when I'm ready.'

She said, 'Yes, but I need to have a shower now so that I can get back to eating Maltesers with Saucy before she wakes up.'

I said, 'I really don't think eating Maltesers with Saucy is going to make any difference to her getting better.'

She said, 'Well, I do, so will you please let me in the bathroom?'

'No,' I said. 'I was here first.'

'Ooooh!'

she screamed.

'You are SO SELFISH!'

My den

So what if I am selfish? I'm the one who's been trying to be nice. I'm the one who wanted to be kind to Gruff. I'm the one who bothered to take him for a run in the park.

And I'm the one who had to go and walk straight into the Dixons …

In bed

Dad said, 'Why don't you tell me what's wrong?'

I said, 'Nothing's wrong.'

He said, 'Well, obviously something is because Sarah said when you went out you were fine but when you came back you definitely weren't.'

I said, 'But I'm telling you I definitely am. And even if I'm not, I'm the one with the problem and I'm the one who's dealing with it.'

He said, 'So there is a problem, then?'

'Well, yes … I mean, no … I mean, it doesn't matter. Nothing does.'

Dad put his hand on my shoulder. 'Everything to do with you matters very much, John,' he said. 'When you want to talk to me, come and talk to me.'

Midnight

Can't sleep. I just keep thinking about them. The Dixons.

I hadn't seen them since last week. I sort of wanted to see them so that I could show them that I was different now – that I wasn't Topzy any more, I was just John. But then again, I sort of didn't want to see them ever again because I kept thinking, what if it made no difference? What if they still looked at me as if I was a scaredy wet fish? What if they still thought I was stupid and pathetic for making God my best friend and trying to live the way He wants me to? What if they only ever saw me as a goody-goody no-hoper?

Well, now I know.

In the park, I threw Gruff's ball for him and he went

pelting off after it, and then I saw them. Or at least I heard them.

'It's Johnny!' yelled Kevin.

'Yeah!' shouted Clyde. 'Johnny and his little dog friend.'

Gruff ran back just as they reached me. I picked him up.

'You always look so scared when you're round us, John,' said Ricky. 'What's that all about?'

'Dunno,' I said. 'I'm not scared of anything.'

'Of course he's not,' said Clyde. 'John doesn't have to be scared because he spends all his time saying prayers with his Topz mates. They say prayers and – bam! – they're all big and brave like big, brave lions.'

'You shouldn't say things like that,' I mumbled.

'Why not?' said Kevin. 'Will it make God angry?'

'Or maybe,' smirked Ricky, 'it'll make <u>you</u> angry and then <u>we'll</u> be the ones who'll need to be scared of <u>you</u>!'

'Actually,' I gulped (I mean, if I was going to tell them, it may as well as be now), 'I'm … not in Topz any more.'

For some reason, that made them all collapse laughing.

'No, I mean it, I'm really not,' I said. 'So just leave me alone.'

I didn't put Gruff down till we were out through the park gate. It wouldn't have mattered if I had, though. They didn't follow me. They carried on doing what they always do. They laughed at me.

And laughed. And laughed.

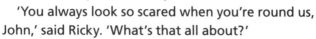

Paul rang.

He said, 'We missed you at the sleepover.'

'Yeah, well, you know how it is,' I said.

He said, 'Oh, you bet. Dave said you must have tons going on because you've got a timetable.'

'Uh huh,' I said.

He said, 'I've got a timetable too, but so far all it's got on it is: Morning – get up.'

'Well, that's a start,' I said.

He said, 'So anyway, I was wondering how you felt about going bowling tonight? Dave's up for it. And Danny. What do you think?'

'I think … no,' I said.

He said, 'Oh, go on, it'll be a right laugh. And it's not a Topz thing. It's just you, me, Dave and Danny. The Nut Crew. Please.'

'No,' I said. 'But thanks anyway.'

My den

What is it about Topzies that makes them refuse to leave you on your own, even though it's unbelievably obvious how much you want to be left on your own? It's as if they have this little radar that sends out emergency and completely wrong 'Topz in trouble' signals and, as soon as they hear the bleeps, they're on the case. And in this case, <u>my</u> case.

beep beep beep beep

I was in my den, looking at a leaflet I picked up yesterday about a summer (wet season) holiday cricket club and wondering whether to get Dad to ring the number and see if I could join, when who should knock on my den door but Dave and Danny.

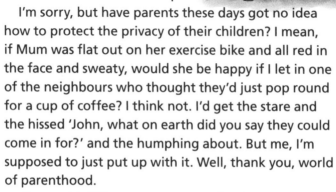

Dave said, 'Hi, John. Your mum said it was OK to come on up.'

I'm sorry, but have parents these days got no idea how to protect the privacy of their children? I mean, if Mum was flat out on her exercise bike and all red in the face and sweaty, would she be happy if I let in one of the neighbours who thought they'd just pop round for a cup of coffee? I think not. I'd get the stare and the hissed 'John, what on earth did you say they could come in for?' and the humping about. But me, I'm supposed to just put up with it. Well, thank you, world of parenthood.

Dave said, 'What are you up to, then?'

'Just planning ahead for the wet season,' I said.

'The what?' asked Danny.

'Nothing,' I said.

'Is it looking exciting?' said Dave.

'Depends,' I said.

'On what?' said Danny.

'On what you call exciting, I suppose,' I said.

'Bowling tonight would be exciting,' said Danny, 'but Paul says you don't want to come.'

'So?' I said. 'Is that why you're here?'

Dave looked at Danny. It wasn't any old sort of look, either, it was a 'meaningful' sort of look.

'Oh, what now?' I snapped. 'What is it you want? I've told you I've left Topz, so why don't you leave me alone?'

'That's just it,' said Dave. 'We can't. We know about the Dixons. We know what they've been doing.'

I shrugged as if I couldn't care less. 'What's to know?'

'Ryan saw you,' said Danny. 'He saw you in the park with Gruff on Thursday. He heard what the Dixons were saying.'

I pretended to laugh.

'Good for him,' I spluttered. 'I can't even remember what they were on about.'

'They were on about God,' said Dave. 'You and God. Is that what all this is about?'

I was getting annoyed now. If I wanted to talk about this, I'd find someone and go and talk about it, but I didn't. I REALLY didn't. It was MY situation and I was sorting it. MY way.

'Look,' I said, 'whatever's happening with me and the Dixons, I'm dealing with it. It's cool.'

'It didn't look that way to Ryan,' said Danny. 'And Ryan knows about stuff. He knows what it's like to be picked on.'

'I wasn't being picked on,' I snapped. 'Me and the Dixons, we're fine. In fact, they're not so bad. I reckon they just get funny with us because we're always together – which, let's face it, is a bit pathetic. I think we should all do stuff on our own more.'

'Yeah?' said Dave. 'So that's why you've left Topz, so you can impress the Dixons? Well, if that's how you're feeling then I reckon you need Topz more than ever.'

'Yeah, right,' I said.

'Yeah, right,' said Dave. 'Dixons don't want to make

friends with you. They're out to hurt you. The reason they hate us isn't because we're a gang, it's because of God. What we need to do isn't to go over to their side and start pushing God out. It's to keep on praying for them that they'll get to know God too.'

'What are you talking about?' I muttered. 'I'm not pushing God out.'

'But you're pushing us out,' said Dave, 'and when you stop hanging around with your Christian mates, that's bad news.'

I didn't look at him. I didn't look at either of them.

'You want to know why we don't leave you alone?' said Dave quietly. 'It's because we're your friends and you're part of God's family with us. And we can't leave you alone, otherwise we wouldn't be doing what it says in the Bible.'

'And what's that?' I mumbled.

Dave pulled a folded piece of paper out of his pocket.

'I've written the verse down for you,' he said. 'You can look it up after we've gone.'

I didn't take it so he put it down next to me on the bed.

'We really want you back in Topz,' Danny said. 'If you change your mind about bowling later, ring me up.'

After lunch

It's always the same with Dave. He seems to think he knows it all. All about Topz, all about me, all about God. Just because he's been a Christian the longest, why does that give him the right to tell anyone else what to do?

I'm not pushing God out. I'm <u>not</u>. And what's it got to do with Dave and Danny, or Paul and Benny, or Sarah and Josie, or anyone else in the whole galaxy anyway?

Bathroom

Looked up the Bible verse Dave gave me. Galatians chapter 6, verse 2: 'Help to carry one another's burdens, and in this way you will obey the law of Christ.'

That's it, then. That's why Topz won't leave me alone. They're trying to carry my Dixons burden. They're doing what Jesus wants.

And what am I doing?

★ Me and God ★

Lord God, I know I shouldn't be angry with the Gang because they're only doing what You want them to do. But I want You to know that Dave's wrong. I'm not pushing You out. I'm still talking to You, aren't I? And I heard everything Greg said when he told me I've got to believe that You can make me strong and powerful with Your Holy Spirit even when I feel weak and wobbly. And useless. It's just … with the Dixons … I don't know if You can understand but … I want to do it on my own.

30 JULY — SUNDAY
NON-TOPZ DAY 9

Just got back from church. That showed Dave. That showed all the Topzies. If I was pushing God out, why would I have gone? If I was pushing God out, why would I have volunteered to read the Bible passage at Sunday Club? Or put my hand up to answer every time

Greg asked a question? Or helped clear up at the end and put just about all the chairs away? That's much more than Dave did. He just sat there looking grumpy, then disappeared off with Greg and didn't even put his <u>own</u> chair away. So who's pushing God out now?

1 AUGUST — TUESDAY
NON-TOPZ DAY 11

Saucy is SO much better. She's doing all her normal, annoying things again like trying to catch your shoelaces when you're walking upstairs and hogging all the best cushions, and Sarah said she kept her awake nearly all night last night trying to climb inside her pillowcase. Happy days (and nights).

No Topz visits yesterday.
Or today.
No phone calls, either.
Maybe they've finally got the message.
I'm just John now.

2 AUGUST — WEDNESDAY
NON-TOPZ DAY 12

2.00pm
Still no Topzies. Which is fine. Exactly what I wanted.

Cool, groovy and fantasmagorically wicked.

Bathroom

If only it was as easy to get rid of a twin as it is to get rid of Topz.

I said to Sarah, 'Can I have a go on the exercise bike now?'

She said, 'I've only just got on it.'

I said, 'Yes, but you were on it for hours yesterday, <u>and</u> the day before.'

She said, 'So? I'm on it again now.'

I said, 'So? Why can't it be my turn?'

'Because,' said Sarah, 'I got here first. And anyway, when Mum got this bike, you thought she'd completely lost the plot, so I don't think you actually deserve to go on it at all.'

'YES, BUT I'M BORED! I'VE GOT NOTHING TO DO!'

'WELL, WHOSE FAULT'S THAT?'

Still in the bathroom

Sarah's been banging on the door. She says she's all hot and sweaty now and needs a shower before she goes round to Josie's.

I said, 'I've only just come in here.'

She said, 'But you're <u>always</u> in there.'

I said, 'And?'

She said, 'And? I need a shower because I smell!'

I said, 'Tell me something I don't know.'

She shouted, 'Why do you have to be so mean about every single tiny thing? I need a shower because I'm going out, and if it wasn't for you I wouldn't be having to go out in the first place!'

'What's that supposed to mean?' I demanded.

'Nothing,' she said.

'It obviously means something or you wouldn't have said it.'

'It doesn't … So, are you going to let me in or not?'

'Not.'

3.00pm

I said to Mum, 'Why's Sarah gone round to Josie's?'

Mum said, 'Why does Sarah ever go round to Josie's?'

I said, 'But what do they have to talk about all the time?'

Mum said, 'What do girls normally talk about?'

I said, 'Has it got anything to do with me?'

Mum said, 'Why should it have anything to do with you?'

I said, 'Do you have to keep answering my questions with another question?'

She said, 'Is that what I'm doing?'

My den

Urgh. In fact urgh, urgh and urgh.

Bathroom

I don't think I've ever been this bored.

My den

Come to think of it, I don't think I've ever not spoken for this long.

Bathroom

Except when I'm asleep.

My den

But then most people don't talk when they're asleep.

Bathroom

Unless they're talking in their sleep, I suppose.

Sarah's room

Saucy's head's inside Sarah's pillowcase. She looks bored as a mushroom, like me.

My den

How on earth much longer is Sarah going to be round at Josie's for anyway?

Sarah's room

Oh, this is rubbish. I'm going out.

In bed much later

⭐ **Me and God** ⭐

I'm sorry, Lord. I'm just really, really sorry …

3 AUGUST – THURSDAY

6.00am

The trouble with trying to do things without God is that you get them wrong. How could I have got everything SO wrong?

My room

Sarah said, 'It's OK, you know. Everyone gets things wrong sometimes.'

But this was big. Really, really big. HUGE.

When I went out yesterday, I didn't take Gruff. I thought I'd just kick a ball around on my own. Anything was better than staring at the walls. 'Sage Moment' was beginning to look more and more like 'Slimy Frog'. 'Slimy, Bored Frog'. 'Slimy, Bored, I'm-so-sick-of-my-own-company Frog'.

I was dribbling the ball around the goalposts when I heard them. Topz. I looked round and they were just going into the skateboard park. All of them. Even Sarah and Josie were there so they must have come to the end of whatever they were nattering on about.

Dave saw me and waved, and Benny yelled over, 'Yo! John! How's it going?'

'Great!' I yelled back. 'It's all going great.'

But they didn't call me over. They didn't ask if I wanted to join in. They just got on with messing about on their boards. Which was fine, obviously, because I didn't want to go over anyway, and if they'd asked me I would have said no.

But they didn't ask me. They just didn't. And I didn't go over.

Trouble was, I felt a bit of an idiot with them over there and me over here. I didn't know if they were watching me. Messing about on their skateboards but all the time thinking what a tragic little ex-Topz I was.

Only it wasn't Topz who thought I was tragic.

It wasn't Topz who caught up with me by the park

gates on my way home.

It wasn't Topz who made me do the worst thing I've ever done in my life.

It was the Dixons.

'Oi! John! Where's the fire?'

That was Clyde.

'What?' I said.

'Why are you running away? We were just going to come over and share your football.'

'Oh,' I said. 'Well, sorry, but I've got to go.'

'Got to go where?' said Kevin. 'If you're looking for your little Topzy mates, we just passed them in the skateboard park.'

'I know where they are,' I said, 'but like I told you, I've moved on from that. I'm not in Topz any more.'

'Hang on a sec, I get it!' grinned Ricky. His face was all lit up as if someone had just given him the biggest ice cream that ever saw the inside of a cornet. 'They're in the skate park. You're on your own with a football. They don't want you any more, do they, Johnny? They've chucked you out!'

I shook my head. 'No! It was up to me. I'd just had enough of it. I wanted to be just John. I'm quite happy being just John. I'm good on my own.'

But I was lying. I wasn't happy being just John at all. In fact I was getting sick of it. And maybe Ricky was right. Maybe the Gang did want me back for a while, but now they'd got used to me not being around, they didn't care. They probably even liked it better without me. That's why they never invited me to go skateboarding. That's why they didn't call me over.

And that's why I was stuck on my own in the park

gateway with Dixons breathing down my neck.

Clyde came a step closer.

'Prove it,' he said.

I didn't know what he meant.

He said, 'If you've really left the Topz Gang … prove it.'

'I'm telling you that's what's happened,' I shrugged. 'How can I prove it?'

They were all standing round me. I was pretty well backed into the hedge. I saw Clyde glance round at the others. They all had those horrible smirks on their faces. Whatever they were planning, there wasn't a lot I could do about it.

But, as it turned out, they weren't planning to do anything themselves. Their idea was to get me to do it for them.

'I'll tell you how you can prove it,' hissed Clyde. 'If you've <u>really</u> left Topz, how about you go and do something for Dixons?'

'Like … what?'

'Well, I don't know about you lot, but I'm starving. You could go and get us something to eat. What d'you reckon, Ricky?'

'Sounds good to me,' said Ricky.

'And me,' said Kevin. 'I want crisps.'

For a second I was relieved. I thought they were going to ask me to go and do something bad. Something I could get in real trouble for. I was the one smiling now.

'I would,' I said. 'I fancy some crisps myself, but I can't get you any. I haven't got any money.'

There was silence. They were all staring at me. They weren't even laughing. And that's when I realised. They <u>were</u> asking me to go and do something bad. Whether I had money or not didn't make any difference. They wanted me to go into a shop and just take something.

I didn't know what to do. I was on my own. Me and the Dixons. Even if I'd been closer to the skate park, I couldn't have shouted out to the Gang for help. How could I ask them for anything now when all I'd been doing was pushing them away? Not only that, but if I did call to them, the Dixons would <u>never</u> believe me about not being in Topz. They'd never see me as just as tough as they are. And they'd never leave me alone.

So I did it. I did this really, really, REALLY AWFUL thing. I told myself, maybe it's not so bad. There's loads of stuff in that shop. They're hardly going to miss a couple of bags of crisps. And it's not as if I'm pinching them for me, I'm giving them away. Maybe God won't notice. After all, it's just one wrong thing.

I left the Dixons outside by the buckets of flowers on the pavement and went into the newsagents on my own. Mr Mallinson was busy serving an old lady wearing a rain hat and carrying an umbrella.

She obviously knew it was the wet season, too. There were four people behind her in a queue, so I guessed Mr M would be busy for a few moments at least. Mrs Mallinson was … I don't know, I couldn't see her anywhere.

So I thought, just do it now. Really quick. There's no one looking. As soon as those people at the counter leave, you've got no chance. It's now or never.

I stood in front of the crisps. There were bags and bags of them. And it's surprising how big and bulky a bag of crisps looks when you suddenly realise that all you've got to hide it in is your jeans' pocket.

My mind started whizzing. What was I going to do? The lady with the rain hat had gone and the next person in the queue was just leaving. I had to grab something right now or Mr Mallinson would spot me for sure. Were the Dixons watching? I didn't know. I didn't care any more. All I wanted was to get out of there. To be at home. In my room. Sitting on the garden wall with Dad. Even arguing with Sarah over whose go it was on the exercise bike would be better than being here. Hovering guiltily in a shop. Doing what I was about to do.

'Thanks, see you soon, Geoff,' Mr Mallinson was saying.

The next thing I heard was a crinkly, crunching sound. It was the noise a bag of cheese and onion crisps made as my fingers closed clumsily round it. It seemed so loud I thought the whole of Holly Hill must have heard it. The whole of England. The whole world.

I turned, still trying to stuff the bag into my pocket, and headed for the door.

I was almost there.

I was going to make it.

Then she stopped me. Mrs Mallinson. She'd appeared out of nowhere. Her voice rang horribly through the quiet, little shop.

'Excuse me, young man, but have you got something in your pocket?'

My heart was thumping. It didn't seem to be in my chest any more, it was in my throat. I thought I was going to choke. I couldn't even breathe.

Outside the door, I was vaguely aware of Dixons shoving each other out of the way as they ran off, squealing and laughing.

But then I saw someone else. I saw Dave. Then Benny. Even Sarah. They were all there, the whole Topz Gang, staring in at me through the door. Gazing at me with sad faces. Watching me stealing something.

'Well?' demanded Mrs Mallinson. 'Are you going to speak to me or shall I have a look in your pocket myself?'

I don't really know what happened next. I remember starting to feel very sick and wondering what on earth Mum and Dad would say when Mr Mallinson phoned them up to tell them they'd caught a thief in their shop and that the thief was me. I remember hearing Dave burbling on about 'sorry' and 'didn't mean to cause any trouble' and 'here's the money for the crisps' and 'it's just been a bit of a misunderstanding' and 'I promise it won't ever happen again'. I remember Sarah looking lost and worried and murmuring, 'I've always thought this is a stupid thing to say, but you honestly do look as white as a sheet.' And I remember walking up to the front door of Dave's house with him and going up to his room.

But how it happened that I didn't get into a whole heap of nasty trouble, I don't remember that at all. I just know it was down to Topz.

'Here,' said Dave, and gave me a big glass of fizzy lemon. It was icy cold.

He was quiet for a moment.

Then he said, 'They're bad news, you know, Dixons. Like I said before, all they're really out to do is hurt you.'

I nodded. I still couldn't speak so I just nodded.

'It's funny how God works things out,' he went on. 'I've been worrying about you, you see, not knowing what to do, and I was talking to Greg after Sunday Club. He said that, if you really didn't want to be part of Topz at the moment, the best thing to do was to leave you alone. Just for a bit. He said the more we kept pushing you, the more you wouldn't want to know, which I suppose is what was happening. What we should really be doing, Greg said, was getting together and asking God to help you see how much He loves you and how much you need Him in your life. And how much we all need each other, too.

'So that's what we've been doing. We haven't phoned you. We haven't come round. We've been meeting at Josie's this week and praying for you. Sarah said you were getting really annoyed and she nearly gave it away why she kept disappearing off every day. It just seemed best if you didn't know what we were doing in case it wound you up even more.

'I wanted to call you over earlier when we were skateboarding but Danny said, no, Greg told us we had to let you do your own thing for a little while. Only when we saw the Dixons following you out of the park, we couldn't. We didn't know what was going on but we knew it wouldn't be good. When we got to the shop and heard Mrs Mallinson shouting at you, and Dixons went scarpering off, well … that's when we realised what had happened …'

'What I'd done, you mean,' I said. Whispered, more like.

I started trying to explain, trying to tell Dave how the Dixons made me feel I was useless and pathetic because I hung around with Topz and spent time talking to God. I tried to tell him that it wasn't that I'd wanted to leave the Gang, it's just that I'd wanted the Dixons to see me as someone brave. Someone strong. Someone who was good on his own. Someone who didn't need anyone else. I'd even got myself believing it. I even thought I could sort it without God.

And the worst part is, the very, very worst part is that I let God down. I didn't stand up for what's right. When all those people turned against Jesus, it would have been so easy for Him to run away, to say, 'Yes, you're right, I'm making it all up' – anything to save Himself. But He didn't. Like Dad told me, Jesus stuck to the truth. Jesus stuck to what He knew was right and to what God wanted, no matter how much it was going to hurt Him.

I kept thinking, maybe it was easier for Jesus. He's the Son of God. He's ... special. Different. It must have been easier for Him to stand up for God than it is for me. But really it wouldn't have been, would it, because when He lived on earth, He was like us. That's the whole point, Jesus was just like us. If He had any power to see everything through, God gave it to Him because He asked for it. But me, I didn't even bother to ask for His help.

Suddenly Dave said, 'But it's going to be OK now, you fruitcake, because you've worked it out. Things are sorted in the shop. Mr and Mrs Mallinson said they'd let it go this time because you've never done anything like it before. Anyway, they spotted Dixons outside so they had a pretty good idea who put you up to it. Everything can get back to normal.'

'But what colour's normal?' I mumbled. All I could still see was dark bluey-black.

'Sorry?' said Dave.

I shook my head. 'It doesn't matter. Anyway, how can everything get back to normal? Look at what I've done. Look at how I've been. I'm out of the Gang and I can't see how God'll ever forgive me even if I ask Him to.'

'You just don't get it, do you?' Dave said. 'First of all, you <u>are</u> in the Gang. You were never <u>out</u> of the Gang. Why else do you think we've been worrying about you? Why else would we bother praying for you? We're a family. God's family. We look out for each other. God understands about feeling frightened. He understands about feeling useless and pathetic, and that's why He gives us family and friends to help us. That's why we have to keep talking to each other so we know what's going on.

'And second of all, if anyone says to God that they're sorry for things they've done wrong, He FORGIVES them. It doesn't matter what it is. It can be something silly like having a pointless argument with Sarah, or something like stealing. It makes no difference to God. There aren't some sins that He will forgive and some that He won't. We all do things wrong all the time. We all need God to forgive us. And we can all be forgiven as long as we're really, truly sorry and do our best not to do those wrong things again. Have you got that?'

'That's actually quite scary,' I said. 'You sound exactly like Greg.'

'Good,' Dave said. 'Then listen to Greg and stop being such a bean bag.'

4 AUGUST — FRIDAY

Been sitting on the garden wall with Dad.

He said, 'Choose a car colour, then.'

I said, 'Actually, would it be all right if we didn't do car spotting today? I wondered if we could just … chat.'

'Just chatting would be great,' said Dad.

'Well, it's like this,' I said. 'Dave says that if we're really and truly sorry for what we've done wrong, God will forgive us. Even for really, really bad things, because to God sin is sin and it's all really, really bad.'

'Dave's absolutely right,' Dad said. 'God does forgive us if we're really sorry. But we need to repent of the things we've done wrong as well. Repenting means being sorry and then turning right away from them.

Turning our back on the bad things and doing our best to live how God wants us to.'

'And when we do that,' I said, '<u>properly</u> do that, He really forgives us, does He? God really wants us back as His friends again?'

'Of course He wants us back!' Dad smiled. 'He wants everyone back! Every single person on this planet, because He loves every single person on this planet. Including you.'

'Yeah,' I said.

'Do you know that story Jesus told about the lost son?' Dad asked. 'A man had two sons, and the younger one went to his dad and said, "After you die, I will get half of everything you own, your land and your money. Only, I'd like the money now." The man loved his son very much, so although it made him sad, he gave him what he asked for. With all that money in his pocket, his son got up and left home. He went a long way away and started living a very empty, selfish life and using his money for lots of bad and wasteful things.

'Then, one day, all that money ran out. He had nothing left to live on and the only job he could get was wading around in mud looking after pigs. Even the pig food looked good to him because he was so hungry. He was very lonely and he was very unhappy, and that's when he came to a decision. He decided he would go back home, tell his dad how sorry he was for being selfish and for wasting all his money, and ask his dad whether he would give him some work so that he could earn a living.

'Now his dad loved his son so much that every day since that son had left, he'd gone outside to watch for

him in case he came home. So when he spotted his son making his way back to the house, he ran over to welcome him.

'His son said miserably, "I'm sorry for everything I've done. I don't deserve to be called your son any more."

'But his dad answered, "What are you talking about? You've never stopped being my son!"

'Then his dad gave him the best clothes to wear, and even put on a welcome home party for him.

'When the older son came home after his day of working for his dad, he was furious to hear what had happened.

'He said, "How could you do this, Dad? I've worked hard for you. I've been good. But my brother went off and left you and was bad. How can you welcome him home? How can you give him fine clothes and a party?"

'And his dad said, "My son, I love you and you have shared everything I have. But your brother, he went away and now he's come back. I lost him, and I've found him again. This party is to celebrate him coming home to our family."'

Dad stopped for a moment, then – 'Do you get it, now?' he asked. 'When we go our own way, chances are things are going to get into a bit of a muddle. But God never stops loving us. God loves us like the father in Jesus' story loved his lost son. He's always waiting for us to come back to Him. He never stops.

PONG

All He wants is for us to ask
Him for forgiveness so that
we can be close to Him again. And when we do ask Him,
He's totally over the moon.'

In bed

TOPZ FOREVER!

Me and God

Youth club was brilliant tonight. I'm a Topzy again,
Lord. Because Topzies are just the absolute topz! I
thought I didn't need them. I thought it was way cooler
being just John. But Topz are like the dad in that story,
too. They watched me do something really bad but they
still welcomed me back. They still want me in the Gang.
And they sorted everything out in the shop with the
Mallinsons. If they hadn't been there, right then, right
at that moment, looking out for me, I don't know what
would have happened.

Thank You for giving me such incredible friends, Lord
God. Friends who know You and want to be the sort of
people You want them to be. Help me to be as good
a friend to them as they've been to me. And help me
never to forget, EVER again, how much I need them.
How much I need other Christians, because they're the
ones who can pray for me. They're the ones who can
help me find my way back to You when I get a bit lost.

I don't care what the Dixons think of me any more,
but I am going to pray for them. Every day. They don't
even know they're lost, yet, but they need to realise so

that they can start to find You, too.

And thank You, Lord, for forgiving me. Thank You that You love me so much even though I don't deserve Your love at all.

You wanted me back.

You've welcomed me home.

And that's the only place I want to be.

Amen.

Collect the set:

Christians needn't be boring
Benny's Barmy Bits
ISBN: 978-1-85345-431-8

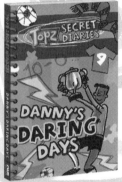

Confidently step out in faith
Danny's Daring Days
ISBN: 978-1-85345-502-5

You can always talk to God
Dave's Dizzy Doodles
ISBN: 978-1-85345-552-0

The Holy Spirit helps us live for Jesus
Gruff and Saucy's
Topzy-Turvy Tales
ISBN: 978-1-85345-553-7

You can show God's love to others
Josie's Jazzy Journal
ISBN: 978-1-85345-457-8

Keep your friendships strong
Paul's Potty Pages
ISBN: 978-1-85345-456-1

You are special to God
Sarah's Secret Scribblings
ISBN: 978-1-85345-432-5

IF YOU LIKED THIS BOOK, YOU'LL LOVE THESE:

TOPZ

An exciting, day-by-day look at the Bible for children aged from 7 to 11. As well as simple prayers and Bible readings every day, each issue includes word games, puzzles, cartoons and contributions from readers. Fun and colourful, *Topz* helps children get to know God.
ISSN: 0967-1307
£2.75 each (bimonthly)
£14.95 UK annual subscription (six issues)
Prices shown are correct at time of printing.

TOPZ FOR NEW CHRISTIANS

Thirty days of Bible notes to help 7- to 11-year-olds find faith in Jesus and have fun exploring their new life with Him.
ISBN: 978-1-85345-104-1

TOPZ GUIDE TO THE BIBLE

A guide offering exciting and stimulating ways for 7- to 11-year-olds to become familiar with God's Word. With a blend of colourful illustrations, cartoons and lively writing, this is the perfect way to encourage children to get to know their Bibles.
ISBN: 978-1-85345-313-7

For current prices visit www.cwr.org.uk

National Distributors

UK: (and countries not listed below)
CWR, Waverley Abbey House, Waverley Lane, Farnham, Surrey GU9 8EP.
Tel: (01252) 784700 Outside UK (44) 1252 784700 Email: mail@cwr.org.uk
AUSTRALIA: KI Entertainment, Unit 21 317-321 Woodpark Road, Smithfield,
New South Wales 2164. Tel: 1 800 850 777 Fax: 02 9604 3699
Email: sales@kientertainment.com.au
CANADA: David C Cook Distribution Canada, PO Box 98,
55 Woodslee Avenue, Paris, Ontario N3L 3E5. Tel: 1800 263 2664
Email: swansons@cook.ca
GHANA: Challenge Enterprises of Ghana, PO Box 5723, Accra.
Tel: (021) 222437/223249 Fax: (021) 226227 Email: ceg@africaonline.com.gh
HONG KONG: Cross Communications Ltd, 1/F, 562A Nathan Road, Kowloon.
Tel: 2780 1188 Fax: 2770 6229 Email: cross@crosshk.com
INDIA: Crystal Communications, 10-3-18/4/1, East Marredpalli,
Secunderabad – 500026, Andhra Pradesh. Tel/Fax: (040) 27737145
Email: crystal_edwj@rediffmail.com
KENYA: Keswick Books and Gifts Ltd, PO Box 10242-00400, Nairobi.
Tel: (254) 20 312639/3870125 Email: keswick@swiftkenya.com
MALAYSIA: Canaanland, No. 25 Jalan PJU 1A/41B, NZX Commercial Centre,
Ara Jaya, 47301 Petaling Jaya, Selangor. Tel: (03) 7885 0540/1/2
Fax: (03) 7885 0545 Email: info@canaanland.com.my
Salvation Book Centre (M) Sdn Bhd, 23 Jalan SS 2/64, 47300 Petaling Jaya,
Selangor. Tel: (03) 78766411/78766797 Fax: (03) 78757066/78756360
Email: info@salvationbookcentre.com
NEW ZEALAND: KI Entertainment, Unit 21 317-321 Woodpark Road,
Smithfield, New South Wales 2164, Australia. Tel: 0 800 850 777
Fax: +612 9604 3699 Email: sales@kientertainment.com.au
NIGERIA: FBFM, Helen Baugh House, 96 St Finbarr's College Road, Akoka,
Lagos. Tel: (01) 7747429/4700218/825775/827264 Email: fbfm@hyperia.com
PHILIPPINES: OMF Literature Inc, 776 Boni Avenue, Mandaluyong City.
Tel: (02) 531 2183 Fax: (02) 531 1960 Email: gloadlaon@omflit.com
SINGAPORE: Alby Commercial Enterprises Pte Ltd, 95 Kallang Avenue #04-00,
AIS Industrial Building, 339420.Tel: (65) 629 27238 Fax: (65) 629 27235
Email: marketing@alby.com.sg
SOUTH AFRICA: Struik Christian Books, 80 MacKenzie Street, PO Box 1144,
Cape Town 8000. Tel: (021) 462 4360 Fax: (021) 461 3612
Email: info@struikchristianmedia.co.za
SRI LANKA: Christombu Publications (Pvt) Ltd, Bartleet House,
65 Braybrooke Place, Colombo 2. Tel: (9411) 2421073/2447665
Email: dhanad@bartleet.com
USA: David C Cook Distribution Canada, PO Box 98, 55 Woodslee Avenue,
Paris, Ontario N3L 3E5, Canada. Tel: 1800 263 2664 Email: swansons@cook.ca

CWR is a Registered Charity – Number 294387
CWR is a Limited Company registered in England – Registration Number
1990308